DIVISIBLE

A POLITICAL NOVELLA

RANDY ANDERSON

Cover design by ebooklaunch.com

This is a work of fiction. Names, characters, businesses, places, events and incidents are either the products of the author's imagination or used in a fictitious manner.

ISBN: 1544802854
ISBN-13: 978-1544802855

ACKNOWLEDGMENTS

Super special thanks to my beta readers: Francine Ferguson, Scott Hirschfeld, Mauro Melleno, Suzette Porte, and Debbie Courtney Anderson–aka mom! I'm so glad I had your support and encouragement. This book grew from your faith in me.

To the resisters who demand from our country better leaders, better laws, and a more tolerant society. May the fictions within this book remain fictions and the truths shown the light.

di·vis·i·ble

dəˈvizəb(ə)l/

adjective
adjective: **divisible**

capable of being divided

Chapter 1

Debriefing Notes
North American Trade Summit
Jackie Hope, Chief Minister of Trade for the United State

Every time I feel the plane make that sharp left turn over the Columbia region of the United State, I'm overwhelmed by a combination of relief and sorrow. The relief comes from knowing that I'm once again flying over my own country, not that there's anything particularly frightening about flying over Canada. But in these divisive times, there is something comforting about being in your own land. The sorrow comes because this turn is required of the pilot. The shortest route from Boston to San Francisco isn't across six Canadian provinces followed by a sharp left and down the West Coast. It's over the heartland of North America. A landmass that has been, for my forty-two years of life, enemy territory.

Shared airspace would be a major victory, not only for relations between the United State and America, but also for the environment. Approximately seventeen million gallons of fuel are wasted on this circuitous route every year, and this is something my colleagues in the Department of Environmental Conservation chant on an almost daily basis. Their pleas haven't fallen on deaf ears. The Department of Transportation and the Military have been working on the problem for decades; better fuel efficiencies and solar flight have also been topics of discussion. But these technologies have been slow to come. And even when they do, we still lose the time and the money we pay the Canadians for crowding their sky.

The ideal solution is to fly directly across America. But that, simply put, has been too difficult a negotiation. America is convinced they have all the leverage, that they have the United State over a barrel; and I suppose they do. Their country sits like a moat, physically dividing our people.

Someday, my superiors tell me, we will possess something of enough value so as to broker airspace permissions. I've been convinced my entire life that we already do. We have a very comfortable egalitarian society. Our way of life and the systems we've put in place to make this way of life possible is worth an unquantifiable amount. Why not share with them our systems and bring them into the modern world? But that, I'm told, is my cultural bias. The Americans have no interest in our way of life. My job is to secure a trade agreement, not colonize another nation. So I swallow my biases and endure an additional two hours in the air.

My itinerary is as follows: depart from Boston on Monday, arrive in San Francisco and immediately board the train to the International Customs House in Lake Tahoe. This is the only boarder passage between our two countries, intentionally placed, I believe, for maximum inconvenience to the people of the Northeast. Of course, the proximity to the land we claimed at the end of the war could also be the reason. Regardless, if I were from any other country, I wouldn't need to fly across the continent to cross the border. But just as they are my enemy, I am theirs.

After what is sure to be a very thorough search and interrogation process—I've only done it once and it took seven hours—I will board a chartered bus for the capital of America, Houston. I have clearance to be in Houston for one day. Regardless of whether more time is needed, I must depart Houston no later than Thursday. Arrangements have been made to travel by an American boat from Houston to Cuba, where I will spend the weekend relaxing before taking the first flight from Havana to New York the following Monday.

Why would the American Trade Captain summon me so suddenly? He and I have been attempting to work out a great number of trade deals for over seven years. Our predecessors, while brilliant statesmen, had left us in such deep trenches that we were required to move copious quantities of earth just so our eyes could meet. Once the herculean task of burying our misconceptions, fears and mistrust was complete, and we could finally square off on even ground, we discovered an unfortunate reality. Truth shines a bright light on a fearless trust, and the truth was that both our countries held such distaste for each other that doing business would be like eating one another's shit. These were the Trade Captain's words, not mine. I preferred to describe the situation as lying with an undesirable lover. And doesn't that just sharpen the point.

So it was certainly a surprise when I received a correspondence from Trade Captain Tom Johnson requesting my presence in Houston to discuss a comprehensive trade deal between America and the United State. Any sort of trade deal between our countries has eluded every diplomat since the war ended. It would be a monumental step toward improving relations. While I'm certain this trip will amount to nothing more than a week of missing my wife and two daughters, it is my duty to hold on to optimism like a torch on a moonless night. After all, without the light of optimism, one cannot navigate through dark times.

While I won't hold out hope for a more direct cross-continental flight, I am curious to know what rich new offer the Americans will have for us. It certainly won't be energy. They tried to convince the United State that their cheap natural gas, oil and ethanol were irreplaceable resources. We responded by outlawing the burning of fossil fuels for everything other than aerospace. Then we implemented a hyper-smart grid—two actually, east coast and west coast—fueled entirely by the sun and the moon. And when the Southwest began its multi-decade drought—hastened no doubt by those "irreplaceable resources"—it was water they offered. Once again, our response was to exercise independence. We built not one but seven of the world's largest desalination plants. The Pacific Ocean now produces so much fresh water that we're making glaciers in the mountains to store it all. Water, I'm sad to say, is about the only resource the oceans have left to give.

While I'm proud of these accomplishments, I do wish we'd been able to make these strides with our American neighbors. After all, we must begin working together at some point, mustn't we? But their price remains too high and always requires the forfeiture of land. Whether it's the eastern side of Lake Erie, where the hills are rich with natural gasses, or the valleys of the West Coast, where the agricultural output dwarfs that of half the planet, they're always looking to expand their map.

They came close to acquiring the northeastern section of the West Coast; with its fertile fruit valleys and rolling wheat fields in the rain shadow of the Cascade Mountains. This, they said, was rightfully their land and that their people were suffering a great injustice being forced to endure our way of life. While nobody disputes them on that point, the Americans grow quiet when the same argument is made for the millions of people in their cities living under their regime. Thousands of United State sympathizers are incarcerated or killed every year, trying to escape the urban ghettos of America.

Nevertheless, we listened to their reasoning and to the people of the Palouse, who put the issue to a district vote. The exchange was set up as 600 square miles of the Palouse region all the way to the Wenatchee valley, currently part of the United State, for two restricted commercial air traffic routes, a northern and southern passage directly across the continent. The district vote was split 50–50, with a tiny fraction of the majority opting to leave the United State and join America. Unfortunately for the United State, but—in my opinion—fortunate for the people of the Palouse, America pulled the deal off the table when their friends in Russia offered a generous arrangement on their abundant supply of wheat, diluting the value of the land on offer. The Russians continue to bolster their special relationship with America, much to the dismay of the rest of the world.

I'm given great latitude in my negotiations, but ever since the near concession of the Palouse, land is strictly off limits. The United State will neither concede nor trade away any property. Goods—both grown and manufactured, technologies, and even human resources are all fair negotiating items. But the only territory I am authorized to discuss in any way is the airspace above America. And that, as I've already stated, is not something they are willing to give up without tremendous concessions from us.

It is possible that the Americans have found fresh trouble with their South American trading partners. Their relationship with Russia has always strained trade with Europe. And, while both the United State and America have good trade relations with most Asian countries, geography slows the delivery to a country with no Pacific ports. If they're not going to let us fly over their land, we won't assist with the delivery of their rare earth materials and rice.

This is why South America has been a crucial component of their trading strategy. America's auto manufacturing has proven an invaluable asset for the entire Southern Continent. Their hunger for automobiles is so great that they'd be willing to trade their children for four wheels. Naturally, they're not swapping babies for Fords, but they do ship everything from seafood and wine to textiles and timber north, across the Gulf of Mexico.

Many countries in South America are prone to frequent unrest. While the people want their cars, their governments sometimes withhold the supply as an act of control. Violence breaks out and there is bloodshed. These uprisings are fueled by America's second largest export, munitions. Naturally, these governments are not pleased when the Americans sell guns to their people on the black market. But for the Americans, it makes good business sense.

Naturally, playing both sides is risky, and if America's trading relationship with any one of the thirteen countries that constitute the South American Trading Pact were to falter, there would be a tremendous shortage of supplies in America. And if, for some reason, the entire Pact were to suspend its shipments, I suspect half of America would starve to death within a year. I wish I were being hyperbolic, but American corporations opted for quick profit over sustained supply, and as a result, they polluted their farmland into oblivion.

Surely, if something of that gravity were taking place, I'd have heard about it. So I doubt I was called to discuss filling a South American trading void. But there was an undeniable urgency to the Trade Captain's message. And why the need for a visit? If it were simply another pass at a low-level trade agreement, we could have video-conferenced. Even a multi-faceted trade agreement could be discussed through technology.

Travelling from one country to the other is a difficult endeavor, especially for high-ranking officials. It requires governmental approval from the highest levels, including signatures from both Presidents. And each President demands to see the other's signature before adding their own. It's a ridiculous game that can take up to a month to complete. My papers, however, were signed and delivered in seventy-two hours. If anyone documents such things, I'm certain this was a record.

Presumably, our leaders know what this trip is about. I would hope that my President didn't just sign me passage into a hostile territory without knowing their intentions. As of right now though, I've not been made aware of anything more than my itinerary.

I asked my superior for a more thorough briefing so that I could better prepare for the meeting, but was told it wouldn't be necessary. I was already adequately prepared for the meeting. In fact, they told me I was the ideal candidate.

"The ideal candidate?" I asked him. "Anyone can be blindfolded and tossed into a room full of hyper masculine white men. You don't need the Chief Minister of Trade to excite these people. They'll eat anything."

He laughed. "We're not chumming the waters, Jackie. You know your way around the Americans. We might have a unique opportunity here and the window is small. We need you to show up and listen to their proposal."

"Then what?" I asked.

"You'll have a few minutes to consider it. And then, you'll need to make a decision before you leave the room."

Beginning our descent into the glorious city of San Francisco, I ruminate on this final directive. I'm certain that many important decisions have been made in a matter of minutes. Certainly, the people of Ute made their world-changing decision in as short a time. But I'm not accustomed to working at such speeds. Governmental negotiation is a slow and delicate art. It is not something to be performed in the triage tents of a battlefield. Medics save lives in minutes. Diplomats save civilizations over years, decades, centuries even.

Chapter 2

Official Court Transcripts
4th Circuit Family Court, America
Pelham vs. Pelham
In the matter of custodial guardianship of five children:
Tammy Pelham, 17; Jacob Pelham, 10; Donald Pelham, 8;
Betsy Pelham, 4; and William Pelham, 2.

ATTORNEY FOR THE PLAINTIFF: Mr. Pelham, please introduce yourself for the court.

JOHN PELHAM: Sure. My name is John Pelham. I was born and raised here in St. Louis. I'm… a… I'm thirty-nine years old. I'm currently employed by Perfect Environment Heating and Cooling. I work as their Chief Mechanical Engineer. Been there for twenty-two years. I started as a tech assistant and worked my way up.

ATTORNEY FOR THE PLAINTIFF: Thank you, Mr. Pelham. That's very impressive. Will you please describe for the court—in your own words—your relationship with your children?

JOHN PELHAM: Gosh, I'd be happy to. I mean, I love talking about my kids. What father doesn't, right? First of all, I want the court to know that my children are the single most important people in my life. Period. I treasure them above everything else. I just can't emphasis that enough.

Okay, so I guess I'll go in order of age. First is my eldest daughter, Tammy. She's been such a wonder to me. She's a really tenacious... is that the word? I think that's the word. Tenacious. She's really... persistent. That's the word. She's persistent. Never stops workin' at something till she gets it done. On second thought, I shouldn't say she's a wonder either. A wonder is some big mysterious thing like the pyramids of Egypt or something. She's not mysterious like that. She's persistent, but she's not a wonder. Sorry, I'm a little nervous. Never had to speak into a microphone in front of people before. It's makin' it hard for me to find my words... inspiring! That's what she is. She's not a wonder; she's inspirational. I mean, even with all her school and her cheerleading, and the plays she does—she's been the lead in most of them—even with all that, she still manages to help with the chores and take care of the little ones. It can't be easy being the oldest of five, especially since she's so much older. But she doesn't complain about nothin'. Just puts her head down and gets it all done. It's inspiring. She'll be going to college next fall. She's going to study in Atlanta. It's a long ways away and I'm gonna miss her. But I'm real proud. A man couldn't ask for a better daughter. She turned out real good. She'll make an amazing wife someday.

My two oldest sons are Jacob and Donald. They're my best little buddies. Jacob is turning into a real good athlete. He's got the skills for practically every sport under the sun. Track 'n field, football, soccer, baseball, hockey. You name it and he can do it. He even throws a Frisbee better than any ten-year-old I've ever met; well, certainly better than his classmates anyway. Only thing he's got to do is focus, you know. Pick his poison and drink it down. I tell him that every day. I say, "Son, pick your sport, just one, and really go for it." That's the only way he'll get good enough to go pro. Personally, I think he should choose football, not just 'cause it's my favorite sport, but also because it's where there's the most money, and it's the one he's really good at. Lotta boys are good at baseball. But not so many look like football stars when they're ten. But his mother, you know, she's not being helpful. She's been fillin' his head with all sorts of nonsense about how short a football career is and how easy it is to get hurt. You know, it's that kinda talk that keeps good players from being great. No great player ever thought once about getting hurt. Dancers think about getting hurt. Athletes think about being number one. Look, I realize we live in a dangerous world and that other countries want to destroy the American way of life. But we gotta keep moving forward, you know? America is the land of fertile opportunity. America's got balls. Which is why I try and encourage my children, even the girls, to grab the balls, you know. I tell them to grab onto those balls and hold on tight. Seize the opportunities, 'cause you never know when a foreigner is gonna sneak into our country and cut those balls off. Then we'd all be forced to bow down on little carpets or some such nonsense. As Americans, we have to seize the opportunity we've been given. That's how I was raised and that's how I want my children raised.

Now, Donald is a pretty athletic boy too, but he doesn't seem to have the same kinda drive that his older brother does. He likes sports, sure, but for him, it's more like play. And I don't think it's because he's only eight, either. You can just tell. He doesn't have the aggressiveness required of a true athlete. He's more sensitive. He cries a lot. More than a boy his age ought to, if you ask me. But we're working on it and he's gettin' tougher every day.

Four-year-old Betsy is my little angel. She's practicing to be a cook when she grows up. Every time I pass her room, I see her working on some new imaginary dish. She's flipping little pieces of fabric on her pretend griddle and stirring a fresh stew of dirty laundry in her hamper. She's just a sweet as can be. And boy is she quiet and obedient. None of my other kids behave so well. It's her way, I suppose. But I also think it's 'cause she's observant. The quiet ones usually are. She doesn't make any trouble 'cause she watches the others. She knows what gets her mother and me angry. To tell you the truth, we should probably pay more attention to her. A girl who knows how to avoid trouble is often the one who causes the most. Haven't thought about that until just now, but I'm gonna make a note of it. And judge, you have my word, if you grant me custody, I'll be sure to keep a good eye on all my kids, especially the quiet one.

Lastly, I have my newest baby; little boy Billy. I don't know him much yet. While he's got lungs that'll fill the house with sound, he hasn't yet figured how to turn that sound into something that makes any sense. I understand that kids learn things at different times so I'm not rushin' him. When Billy's ready, he'll start talkin'. When he's got something to say, he'll figure out how to make words. Until then, I just gotta love him the same as all the others... maybe give him an extra cuddle at night, so he feels secure. If he gets to feelin' real comfortable, he'll talk. I don't know if that's true or not, but can't hurt to give the boy an extra squeeze before bedtime.

ATTORNEY FOR THE PLAINTIFF: Thank you Mr. Pelham. It sounds like you've built some excellent relationships with your offspring. Now, from a practical point of view, if you were granted custody, can you tell us how you would manage a full-time job and the responsibilities of raising five children?

JOHN PELHAM: Sure. Although, it would really only be four. Tammy will be going to college in Atlanta, so she won't be needing any lookin' after. In fact, she doesn't need any lookin' after now. Come to think of it, she'd be super helpful at home. If I didn't want her to get an education so badly, I'd have her stay here and help raise her siblings. But that's the primitive way, isn't it? America is a modern society. We send our girls to school so they can learn art and science. But to answer your question, I'm pegged to get a big promotion at work. They're gonna make me Regional Director. I won't be going out into the field anymore. It's a desk job, eight to six, with Sundays off. It comes with a big pay raise too. And my boss said that if I get custody, he'll give me every other Saturday off so I can spend more time with my kids. So I'll have more money to spoil them with and more time too. It's a double win.

ATTORNEY FOR THE PLAINTIFF: But what about when you're working? Who will watch the children when you're at the office?

JOHN PELHAM: Oh (inaudible). I didn't answer the question, did I? My mom lives twenty miles away, and she says she'll help out. But my main plan is to hire my buddy's housecleaner, Albina. She's from Russia. My buddy Paul brought her over when she was fifteen, to cook and clean for him. He's a bachelor and has always been pretty useless around the house. He's a damn good mechanic. He can fix your vacuum cleaner, but he sure as hell couldn't use one. And if we're being honest here, my four-year-old is a better cook than Paul. The guy can't even boil water good. Anyway, he's letting Albina go on account that she's getting sloppy. He says its cause she's bored, which I guess is as good a reason as any to go sloppy. Only thing is she doesn't want to go back to Russia. So I said I'd hire her, if I get custody, that is. I doubt she'd be gettin' bored with four kids in the house, and she's twenty now, so she can drive them to their activities and school and stuff. Plus, once Tammy leaves for college, she can have her room. It really is the perfect solution. I'll have a full-time nanny and a part-time grandma. I can't think of a more ideal set up.

ATTORNEY FOR THE PLAINTIFF: Indeed it is. So you've talked about your special relationships with each of your children, and you've outlined how you'll successfully provide food and protection. You're even willing to hire a full-time nanny to ensure stability and routine. These are all wonderful things. Is there anything else, Mr. Pelham, you'd like to share that you feel makes you a better parental figure for your children?

JOHN PELHAM: There sure is. Faith, spirituality and discipline.

ATTORNEY FOR THE PLAINTIFF: Please explain.

JOHN PELHAM: Well, I believe we live our best lives by giving ourselves fully to the glory of the Lord Jesus Christ. That's faith. And if you can let go of all them other distractions that will try and test your faith in Him, His spirit will move through you. And once His spirit is moving through you, you'll be able to distinguish right from wrong. That's spirituality. But it's not enough to simply know right from wrong. It takes a strong will to deny the devil in the wrongs and an unwavering virtue to fly with the angels of the rights. And that is discipline. And I'll tell ya, that's not something they're gonna get from their mother, that's for sure. She'll say she has faith and that she goes to church every Sunday. She may even convince every single person in the congregation that she's the most religious woman on two legs. But I'm here to tell you she's not. And that's coming from someone who knows her better than anyone else. That woman is the least virtuous sack of skin you'll ever meet.

ATTORNEY FOR THE PLAINTIFF: Thank you, Mr. Pelham. That will be all.

JOHN PELHAM: I'm not done. I need to tell you why she's an unfit mother.

ATTORNEY FOR THE PLAINTIFF: Mr. Pelham, we're not here to talk about how unfit she is. That's not what this part is about. We'll get to that later. Right now, we just want to talk about how fit you are to be their father.

JOHN PELHAM: Oh. Well, (inaudible) since she's never done a damned…

ATTORNEY FOR THE PLAINTIFF: That will be all. Thank you for your thoughts, Mr. Pelham. You may step down.

Chapter 3

I wish I could tell you, descendants of mine, exactly what it was that brought us to this point. But if I knew such a thing, I wouldn't be leaving you this note. You see, if I knew, surely many others would have known as well. And I have enough faith in our species, as you should too, to believe that we possess the ability to prevent disaster if only we can see it unfolding. So I must assume that we didn't see it coming.

Perhaps that's too rosy a view of the world. I ask that you grant me this indulgence. You see, I'm writing this letter from a very bleak place indeed. I need to fill myself with all the hope I can summon. Hundreds of feet above me lie some of the most magnificent mountains you'll ever see—evergreen forests spackled with Aspen trees, whose autumn gold makes the landscape appear like the fur of a calico cat. And when the wind blows, the fragile leaves shimmer like tiny tambourines celebrating the last days of their usefulness. And here I sit, hundreds of feet below it all, so far removed from that thin layer of vibrant life on the surface that worms don't dare visit.

Every week, I work a series of twelve-hour shifts. My time off is spent reading and sleeping in the dormitories down the hall, and my weekends are spent hiking through the grandeur of the Rocky Mountains in the glorious Nation of Ute. It's a simple life with a single purpose, and I cherish it.

My job is easy. If the red light on the wall flashes, I press the first button. If it flashes again, I press the second button, and then the third button for the third flash and so on and so forth until all the buttons have been pressed. While I'm curious about what would happen should I press the first button, I possess absolute certainty of the results, were I to press them all.

And that is why I'm writing this communication. I'm asking you, future human, child of my great-great grandchildren's children, to ponder our progress. Whether you look upon these words as a peace offering from the past, a roadmap for the future, or a silly parable offering nothing more than mild entertainment, I urge you read it through and perceive its absolute sincerity.

The troubles of the Old Country are well documented. But we can't blame our forefathers for their experimental follies. They were experimenting, after all. I believe the fabric of any society is built on science, politics, economics, sociology and so forth. These are all sciences, really. And like any scientific experiment, there are failures. In fact, good experimentation demands it. And so we failed, brilliantly, and at great cost to many people. With each failure, we progressed and evolved. A new nation rose between the oceans. A nation governed in a way that allowed a unique freedom. And with this freedom, we first expressed ourselves, then governed that expression. We allowed people the freedom to work hard and grow prosperous and then allowed others to cheat without breaking a sweat. After all, it would be unfair to allow one but not the other, right? We held life in the highest regard, above all else, and then we allowed everyone the tools to take it away. What good is life if it's not constantly in peril? This country grew to understand that true freedom can only exist when good and evil are granted equal audience. Justice, equality and civility were pitted often against piety, tribalism and disrespect.

It wasn't an ideal society. The ideal society is a myth. Societies are born diseased just as surely as the species that comprise them. Sometimes, the pox is a horrendous rash that visibly consumes the victim, destined to seethe in a festering mess of its own puss. Other times though, it's a cancer, hidden for long periods of time. And when it finally grows large enough, it causes symptoms. These are subtle at first—body aches, fevers, and malaise—until finally, when the cancer is discovered, its growth outpaces any attempts to stop it. And while it's true that all societies, like the species they contain, will die, the human being has the unique capacity to extend a single life. So it stands to reason that we have the capacity to extend the life of a society. Civilization building—like medicine—is a science, unfortunately though, without the Hippocratic Oath.

I'll ask you to forgive me if this note digresses from time to time. The darkness of my gray octagonal room creates the illusion of so much space, my mind feels absolutely untethered. The only definitions before me are the soft halo of light around the page on which I write and the damp and eerie glow of the ghost lamp below the red light. It was installed as a safeguard against hallucinations. I will admit, there were times, before the ghost lamp was installed, that I almost believed I saw the red light illuminate. Thankfully it hadn't, and I'm ever grateful to my hands that didn't act upon my eye's lies. Nobody has seen the red light flash since the war ended. And since the ghost lamp was installed, nobody has hallucinated otherwise.

You must know that it was the Nation of Ute that ended the war. There are sure to be historians that will tell a different story, but I have it on good authority that if we hadn't committed that horrible act of treasonous patriotism, the United States of America would have torn itself into a vapor. I am aware that most would look upon an act of treasonous patriotism as nothing more than an oxymoron. But I assure you, there was a moment when an act of treason became a profound display of patriotism. And it was, at the same time, a failure, brilliant, and at great cost to many people.

Unfortunately, the cancer in the United States of America was much too far along. A cure would not be found. And our failure would not make the nation stronger. It only served to stop the war and end the Old Country, leaving two new ones in its place, divided in the most untenable way. It left a remainder—the great Nation of Ute, where I now reside—left free from the governing bodies of both America and the United State by the very buttons that lie before me.

Chapter 4

Debriefing Notes
North American Trade Summit
Jackie Hope, Chief Minister of Trade for the United State

The protests at the San Francisco airport were larger than I'd seen. It's not unusual to see protests anywhere in the United State, especially in urban centers. But this protest was on a much larger scale. And it was situated around the airport rather than a government house or a public park, which made it even more unusual.

I scanned the signs to determine the grievances—as there are always dozens of them—but the moonless evening cast an endless shadow over the throngs of bodies chanting and shouting around me. I was quickly escorted from my plane to our entourage of black vehicles with leather seats and darkened windows. I asked my escort if he knew the protestors' purpose. He simply gave me an annoyed shrug.

"All I know, ma'am, is that they make my job more difficult," he said.

We didn't speak any more about it. It wasn't until I was on the train and had switched the television on that I realized the protestors were there specifically to greet me. In the nine hours that I was in flight, the news of my particular mission had been leaked to the press and the masses assembled.

A large and very vocal majority of United State citizens are extremely suspicious of our neighbors to the south and the east. And whenever we get close to closing any kind of deal with the Americans, the population explodes in protest. Not only is there massive public mistrust, but they also view a trade deal as giving legitimacy to what they believe to be a totalitarian regime. It is their position that human rights trump any convenience a trade deal might bring.

I don't begrudge the protestors presence, unlike my civil escorts. The freedom to assemble, the unfettered freedom of speech, freedom of the press, and the irrevocable right to non-violent civil disobedience are bedrocks of our society, and our citizens use these tools to help shape our rules and steer our governing bodies. Our constitution demands we listen to them, which grants the people power and makes protests quite effective.

But I believe their insistence that we maintain a zero-tolerance policy with the Americans is misguided. We have respectful and even fruitful relationships with other countries with whom we share far less in common. It is my opinion that the more we work together, the more we'll realize how much alike we really are. Taking the first step has been a tremendous challenge. But it's essential if we are to move forward.

At the same time, however, I understand their concerns. The values of our two countries are radically different. I've lost my patience with American officials on more than one occasion, and if I'm being truly honest, if I weren't a high level official, I'd probably be on the streets myself. But I am a high level official, which means I can't physically be on the streets. But, as I watch the news, I see that my name has made it onto every other sign in the crowd. Even a casual glance at the footage shows that these people, the people I'm charged to represent, don't even want me speaking with the Americans, let alone agreeing to whatever deal it is they're willing to make.

I spent the hour-long train ride pouring over the news, looking for clues as to what this deal might consider. But the masses knew only what I did. The Chief Minister of Trade was headed to Houston to broker a deal the Americans feel we cannot pass up. And yet, that alone was enough to spark massive protests across the United State.

Our anger toward the Americans is a deeply buried and fiercely protected emotion, one that would benefit well from an excavation. But the tools for such an endeavor have eluded us for so long we've forgotten what they even look like, let alone how to use them. What if the Americans were offering us a cure for cancer? Would our anger prevent us from accepting such a lifesaving gift? Can we ever possibly shift our feelings from negative to positive? Can distrust morph into acceptance? Hatred into generosity? Fear into gratitude? It's certainly possible for an individual. Why is it so hard for a society?

I moved through the International Customs House with blazing speed. The interview, which felt more like an interrogation, only lasted twenty minutes. Their questions revolved mostly around what I knew of my meeting. Since I knew almost nothing, my answers were quick. I suspect my interviewer had no knowledge either and was using the exercise as a way of extracting information for herself. Besides those probing questions, she stuck closely to her script, focusing on my family, friends and associates. Like my previous visit, the moment I disclosed my relationship to a woman, the tone of the questions changed. Why they don't brief these people before putting them in a room with me is confounding. I'm a fairly well-known figure in both countries. It's no secret that I'm married to a woman. And it's not a crime, even in America, for a woman to be with another woman. It's true they can't marry in America like we can in the United State, but lesbians exist here too. And yet, I'm looked upon as one would observe a mythical creature with a birth defect, like a unicorn with three too many horns.

Because of my disclosure, I was assigned a male attendant for my strip search. They presented this decision as an accommodation to me. They didn't want to make me feel uncomfortable. It is my belief that the women were intimidated by the presence of a strong female—a particularly proud one at that.

I'm fully aware that the purpose of this strip search was to humiliate and that it served no real security purpose. I'd mentally prepared for the exercise and felt no shame or humiliation. In fact, I found their need to place me with a male attendant so ridiculous that I spent the whole time unsuccessfully suppressing my laughter. In the end, it was the most fun I'd ever had being naked with a man present.

The bus the Americans provided was extremely comfortable. The windows extended from the wheel-wells to the ceiling showcasing the tremendous vistas. And what vistas they were! I can honestly say, my two-day journey from Lake Tahoe to Houston was one of the most breathtaking journeys I've ever taken. Winding our way out of the Sierra Nevada mountain range as the sun rose over the Great Basin filled me with such optimism. It wasn't only the splendor of the landscape. There was a brief moment as we descended the mountain, where I felt I was on equal footing with the sun, that somehow I was providing a new dawn for the continent, just as our nearest star. It was a brief moment of private hubris that I occasionally allow myself. No camera could ever capture the sunrise I experienced, so I gave great latitude for the mental imprint.

Traveling through the Mojave Desert offered a wholly different experience, and as the temperatures shot up, the air-conditioning hummed and the windows darkened. I've never been particularly keen on being in drier climates. I prefer the seasonal East Coast over even the mild Mediterranean environment of Los Angles. But something about this trip gave me a new appreciation for the barren beauty of a windswept desert.

Our route took us through America's canyon of buildings in Las Vegas where we craned our heads to marvel at the glittering towers of sin. Then we traveled to the edge of Mother Nature's Canyon, where we bent penitently to spy the river responsible for carving this wonder. We humans inspire awe by making ourselves look upwards. Mother Nature inspires prayer by making us bend down. Our grand tour of the Mojave concluded with a meal as the sun fell over my homeland in the west. The guests of honor arrived in the form of two California condors soaring effortlessly on nine-foot wings, demonstrating an approach to life incomprehensible to us primates.

I slept as we traveled through more mountain ranges. My dreams were visions of the Nation of Ute. Perhaps it was our proximity to the fiercely independent territory; or perhaps it was the ever-changing climate forcing me awake to pile blankets on, only to toss them aside an hour later.

One particular dream had me hiking through the mountains with a group of people who I considered close friends. They were all from the Nation of Ute. I have never seen the Colorado Mountains nor do I have any friends in the Nation of Ute. But there I was in my dream, hiking to the top of an enormous mountain, swapping stories with my loved ones. It wasn't until we reached the peak and were looking down over the Continental Divide that I looked over to my friends and confessed that I was not a member of their tribe. I was not Nation of Ute.

They all had a hearty laugh.

"Jackie," they said, "None of us is truly Nation of Ute. And yet…"

And then I woke up.

I puzzled over this dream all the next morning. The vast and lonely plains of the West South Central region gave space for contemplation, and I used it to unsuccessfully analyze the dream's meaning.

The closer we got to Houston, the stronger my desire to know about this meeting grew. My anxieties were aggravated by the increasing display of poverty that multiplied as we approached America's capital. I've seen the footage and read the statistics. I'm fully aware that almost sixty percent of the American people live in poverty. But seeing it in the flesh was a profound experience.

Tents topped with flimsy solar panels were laid out in a grid that extended from highway to horizon. Children darted through the unpaved streets chased by mothers with babies swaddled on their backs. It was mid-day, so I saw few men. Most would be at work, and those that didn't have a job wouldn't dare show themselves in public. The shame of idleness is too heavy a burden for these proud people.

As we traveled toward the city center, the housing changed. It grew more solid and dense, almost like layers of earth. The outer tents represented the soft and light soil, one hurricane away from extinction. The suburban homes with their sprawling lawns were the red clay just below the surface. The brick townhouses represented the solid quarry stones below that, and finally, the immense and impenetrable bedrock of the inner city with its towers of steel and glass.

It wasn't until we traveled into the more affluent city center that I noticed the windows on the bus dissolving their subtle pink tint. They must have taken on this rose-colored hue slowly as we approached the slums of the outer city. The Americans certainly go out of their way to ensure you see things the way they want you to. They literally hide behind rose-colored glass.

We arrived at my hotel and I was immediately taken to my room on the fifty-seventh floor. The sun was setting on my second day in America. The first was filled with such natural wonder that it was difficult to comprehend any animosity between our countries. But, by the end of day two, seeing the vast inequality forced upon the American people, my mind remembered the sobering reality. The leaders of this land are my enemies of the most profound kind.

Chapter 5

Official Court Transcripts
4th Circuit Family Court, America
Pelham vs. Pelham
In the matter of custodial guardianship of five children:
Tammy Pelham, 17; Jacob Pelham, 10; Donald Pelham, 8;
Betsy Pelham, 4; and William Pelham, 2.

ATTORNEY FOR THE DEFENDANT: Thank you, Mr. Pelham, for your very thorough testimony. It is quite clear that you love your children, and I don't doubt your sincerity when you say they are your world. It's obvious you love them all very much.

JOHN PELHAM: And equally.

ATTORNEY FOR THE DEFENDANT: Yes, and equally. Now, I just have a few questions that I'm hoping you wouldn't mind answering for the court.

JOHN PELHAM: I'd be happy to. That's what we're here for, isn't it? Plus, I'm told that I don't have a choice.

ATTORNEY FOR THE DEFENDANT: Indeed, you don't. Now, you said that if you were granted custody of your children, you would hire your buddy Paul's Russian housekeeper, Albina, to take care of the children.

JOHN PELHAM: And my mother. The kid's grandma will also be helping out.

ATTORNEY FOR THE DEFENDANT: Yes, of course. But the primary guardian will be Albina, your buddy Paul's Russian housekeeper, correct?

JOHN PELHAM: Well, I understood that if I was granted custody, *I* would be the primary guardian. Is that not the case?

ATTORNEY FOR THE DEFENDANT: You'd be the primary parent yes. But a twenty-year-old Russian housekeeper who's good with a vacuum will be the main caregiver for your children, is that correct?

JOHN PELHAM: No ma'am. I will be the main caregiver for my children.

ATTORNEY FOR THE DEFENDANT: Yes, of course. But when you're at work and the children are not with their grandmother, you will hire Albina, Paul's sloppy housekeeper, to look after your offspring, correct?

JOHN PELHAM: Yes. But I don't like how you're describing her.

ATTORNEY FOR THE DEFENDANT: I'm simply using your own words, Mr. Pelham.

JOHN PELHAM: Well I don't think you should...

ATTORNEY FOR THE DEFENDANT: Mr. Pelham, this isn't a discussion. You're here to answer my questions. Now, besides cleaning your buddy Paul's house, are you aware of any other services Albina provides for Paul?

JOHN PELHAM: Sure, she cooks his meals. She does the laundry, makes the bed. Domestic type stuff.

ATTORNEY FOR THE DEFENDANT: So, very similar to the things your wife did around the house before you separated, yes?

JOHN PELHAM: Yeah, I guess.

ATTORNEY FOR THE DEFENDANT: What other things did your wife do for you while you were married?

JOHN PELHAM: I don't know what you mean.

ATTORNEY FOR THE DEFENDANT: Where there any other things your wife did for you, perhaps after the children went to sleep?

JOHN PELHAM: Now, just you wait one minute. If you're insinuating that my wife had sex with me as some kinda chore, like cooking and cleaning, you're dead wrong. That's insulting to me and to her.

ATTORNEY FOR THE DEFENDANT: Indeed, it is. My apologies. But that is one of the chores Albina performs for your buddy Paul, is it not?

JOHN PELHAM: I can't (inaudible). You trapped me!

ATTORNEY FOR THE DEFENDANT: Mr. Pelham, I don't need to trap you. You're under oath, remember? You have to answer all of my questions honestly. Otherwise, you'll be committing perjury. Do you know what that means?

JOHN PELHAM: Yes.

ATTORNEY FOR THE DEFENDANT: Good. Now, please tell the court. Have you ever engaged in sexual intercourse with Paul's housekeeper Albina?

JOHN PELHAM: Yes. But only once. We were drinking. Paul and her started fooling around and then she invited me into her room.

ATTORNEY FOR THE DEFENDANT: Oh, I see. So this wasn't just an affair with Albina. It was an affair with your buddy Paul too.

JOHN PELHAM: No! I said I went into her room. I went after Paul. And it wasn't an affair. I told you, it was one time.

ATTORNEY FOR THE DEFENDANT: But not for your buddy Paul. And isn't it correct that once you hire Albina, Paul is going to hire another fifteen-year-old housekeeper from Russia?

JOHN PELHAM: I don't know what he's gonna do. That's none of my business. But I'm telling you and this court that my having relations with that woman was a one-time thing. I did it, yes. I'm not proud of it. And I've already asked for forgiveness.

ATTORNEY FOR THE DEFENDANT: From whom?

JOHN PELHAM: From God.

ATTORNEY FOR THE DEFENDANT: Perhaps you should have asked forgiveness from your wife? But the point is, Mr. Pelham, you will be hiring a prostitute to watch your children.

JOHN PELHAM: That is absolutely false. I'm not gonna lie and tell you Paul and Albina have had the most appropriate relationship. But I swear to God and the Court, I will not be having any more relations with her. She will be hired to raise my children, nothing more.

ATTORNEY FOR THE DEFENDANT: Mr. Pelham, even if we are to believe that your relationship with Albina would be purely platonic, which I'll admit is rather difficult, I'm curious about your friend. If your buddy Paul is accustomed to sleeping with fifteen-year-old girls, what's to stop him from sleeping with one of your daughters?

JOHN PELHAM: I'd kill him if he did. And right quick too.

ATTORNEY FOR THE DEFENDANT: Wow, Mr. Pelham. Adultery. Murder. You're sounding less and less like a man of God.

JOHN PELHAM: I would do anything to protect my children. And if that means killing my best friend, well then, I'll take it up with God after. But know this, I love my children. I've always done everything I could to protect them and provide for them. And yes, my friend Paul doesn't follow the path of the Lord. But who am I to judge him? All we can do is pray for the lost sheep and hope they find their shepherd soon. But this hearing is about me. And I'm a good man. I'm a hard-working, caring, God-fearing man who will take good care of his children. Remember, I didn't want this divorce. This was her doing. She was the one who decided to defile the vows we took before God and the Church. She was the one who left. We should all remember that. I may not be perfect, but by golly, I was willing to work it out. I was willing to work on our marriage. It was Nancy who left.

ATTORNEY FOR THE DEFENDANT: Yes, she left after she discovered your seventh affair. That's why the judge granted her the divorce, Mr. Pelham, because you're a philanderer.

JOHN PELHAM: I'm not a philanderer! How dare you call me that! Sure, I made mistakes. But those weren't affairs. Those women meant nothing to me. Do you hear me? Nothing. They were simply acts of weakness. One-night stands.

ATTORNEY FOR THE DEFENDANT: Which is the very definition of a philanderer, Mr. Pelham. But, perhaps we should move on. I have a few more simple questions before we're done. When does Tammy get her braces off?

JOHN PELHAM: I don't know. Next year?

ATTORNEY FOR THE DEFENDANT: What is Betsy's favorite food?

JOHN PELHAM: Well… she has lots, I think. Pancakes?

ATTORNEY FOR THE DEFENDANT: What position in football does Jacob want to play? What does Donald want to be when he grows up? What was William's first word?

JOHN PELHAM: I don't know. These kids change their minds about this stuff all the damn time. And what kind of trick question was that? William hasn't said his first word yet.

ATTORNEY FOR THE DEFENDANT: Tammy gets her braces off next week, not next year. Betsy's favorite food is banana pudding, which isn't surprising for a four-year-old. Donald wants to be an astronomer, which is why he's been begging you for a telescope for two years. You say football is your favorite sport, the one you want Jacob to pursue, and yet, you don't know that he's been wanting to play wide receiver since he started; only the coach won't play him. And you should know why.

JOHN PELHAM: Not if Nancy never tells me any of these things. You see, Judge, my wife… my ex-wife, is keeping things from me. She's the real villain here. She doesn't communicate with me. This is why I'm suing for custody. She's been keeping my children's lives from me. And now she wants to physically take them away. You just can't allow it.

ATTORNEY FOR THE DEFENDANT: Has she been keeping things from you? Or, could it be that when these things were happening, you were having emotionally empty intercourse with women who meant nothing to you.

JOHN PELHAM: That's not true. I'm not always having intercourse with women.

ATTORNEY FOR THE DEFENDANT: Yes, you are correct. Not always. Only seven times. I have no more questions for you, Mr. Pelham. But there is one more thing I think you should know. William's first word was "dada." He said it three months ago. But don't let that go to your head. I'm sure he wasn't asking after you. It's practically every baby's first word.

Chapter 6

An open letter to a future generation
Nation of Ute

The last day of the war, the day the Nation of Ute rose up to define itself, was the darkest this continent has ever seen. And that's saying something. Remember, this land has been host to slavery, war and genocide—no small tragedies. But the day the Second Civil War ended was a horror concentrated.

It was late winter and the war was in its seventh month. If it had been a winter of old, perhaps the fighting might have slowed. If only the temperatures dropped and the winds carried snow, people might have stayed warm and safe and left the fighting for another day. But our winters had long grown too mild, making conditions favorable for street combat.

The militias in Detroit and Chicago were pushing toward each other trying to establish control of the Lower Michigan Peninsula, and the United State took advantage of a distracted America to seize the Black Rock Desert all the way up to Paradise Valley. The desert fighting was sparse and involved heavy weaponry; but the battle below the

Great Lakes was a bloody street affair, conducted with handguns and small explosives. Seven thousand people were dying each day on the land between Detroit and Chicago.

Naturally, the fiercest fight was taking place in the capital of the Old Country, Washington D.C. There, both sides fought to control the Capitol, the White House, Senate buildings and monuments. No matter how damaged and bullet-ridden those structures of the Old Country became, both sides were consumed with controlling them, as if occupying those buildings from the past would prove them to be the stewards of the future.

While the people of America and the United State pushed their borders back and forth, a group of citizens quietly moved into the Rocky Mountains. We came from all over the continent, but not in large numbers. Our ideology was mixed; however, we all shared a singular and strong vision—to return peace to this land. We organized as we assembled. We called ourselves the Nation of Ute to honor the indigenous people who originally lived in these mountains.

Our first attempt at peace was to hijack satellites to disrupt the warring factions' communication systems. This, we thought, would slow the pace of the battles. But the task proved extremely difficult. It took three weeks to bring one satellite offline, and the sky was filled with thousands of orbiting machines.

Once we realized that mission would take far too long, we tried using their communication systems to encourage a ceasefire through an information campaign. We bombarded the airwaves with daily statistics on the number of innocent lives that were being lost to the war. We researched and broadcast stories of families being torn apart by misunderstandings, and tried to call out the lies both sides were telling as well. We meant to inspire change, but that too proved useless. The first casualty of the war was the Fourth Estate, and as such, people only consumed news with which they agreed. Trust had become a tribal bond reserved for those who shared your beliefs.

As the Nation of Ute grew and continued to expand its territory, we came across a terrifying and unique opportunity. We were able to thrive in the Rocky Mountains because topography and weather can make it difficult to traverse. This was why the Old Country placed so many of their missiles here. The silos are spread throughout the area, invisible on the surface. In fact, you can walk right over them and never know it. But once we discovered one, we knew what to look for. Soon enough, we'd found three dozen unmanned missile silos containing over three hundred and sixty megatons of nuclear weaponry.

We knew we had to take control of these weapons, but we weren't sure how. That was when Mother Nature provided us with the perfect assist. The air currents shifted, bringing cold air from the north, while a storm from the Pacific sent a tremendous amount of moisture across the mountains. This combination of meteorological events created a massive snowstorm that lasted six days. Over four feet of snow fell in that time. Every road leading into the mountains was impassable. The Continental Divide was completely isolated.

We worked quickly. Our own movements were slowed by the storm, but our population was effectively dispersed.

We had people close to every missile location. Each silo system was hacked, separated from the external communication systems and brought onto a local mainframe. By the time the snow had stopped falling, we had autonomous control of enough weapons of mass destruction to destroy half the continent.

Naturally, our actions drew the attention of both the United State and America. A ceasefire was called in Washington D.C., while the two sides discussed how to deal with this new threat. The Nation of Ute was elated. Our actions were working. We were bringing peace. Of course, the fighting hadn't stopped everywhere. Battles still raged in the Pacific Northwest and along the California border, but it had stopped in the capital, and that was a start.

Sadly, our celebration was nothing more than a public demonstration of naiveté. Four days after the snowstorm passed, the ceasefire abruptly ended, and across the continent, battles devolved into their fiercest fighting yet. Then, the American forces began pushing into the mountains. Our mountains. They approached in caravans from the eastern and western slopes as helicopters dropped troops into remote locations to infiltrate from within. The Nation of Ute was under attack.

An emergency council meeting was held, and the elders spoke quietly and gravely about what we needed to do. While our people fiercely defended our borders and our missiles, the council made its decision.

We stepped outside, turned our heads to the sky and watched as five rockets roared into the heavens. Tears fell fast and hard. Mothers held their children tight. Couples buried their heads in the bosoms of their beloved. This was either a new beginning or the final end. Either way, the moment was so profound, even the forest fell into a silent prayer.

Most victims only had a few minutes warning, which I consider a blessing. The missiles were too fast, and our target too close. All five missiles struck the same target, Washington D.C. The idea was to destroy any notion that the ways of the Old Country were to continue. The past, it seemed, was making it impossible for us to forge a future, and so long as we continued to fight for dominion over that broken system, we'd never find peace.

The city was completely annihilated. We'd underestimated the power of these weapons. Five explosions in a thirty-mile radius turned out to be excessive. The entire world stopped and marveled at the insanity of the people in North America. Over 1.6 million lives perished at the hands of the Nation of Ute.

Five minutes after the explosions, we announced ourselves to the warring nations. The notice was short and transmitted across every known medium.

Dear Citizens of America and the United State,

You have betrayed this land, your country, yourselves and each other. It is clear that your minds will not meet. But we, the Nation of Ute, will no longer allow your swords to. You are on notice. Keep your countries separate and do not war. Any act of aggression will be swiftly met with two missiles, one for each land.

There has been peace ever since.

Chapter 7

Debriefing Notes
North American Trade Summit
Jackie Hope, Chief Minister of Trade for the United State

Breakfast was delivered to my room at 8:00 am—a late start for me as I'd already completed my aerobics, yoga and meditation. I finished showering and got dressed by 7:00 am. I impatiently waited in my room for an hour. Unable to occupy my mind with anything other than speculation of the coming day, I paced along the floor-to-ceiling windows looking out over the vast city. The weather was clear, but the haze of pollution prevented me from seeing the Gulf of Mexico, something I'm not even sure would be possible on a smog-free day.

Once again, the Americans were not properly briefed about me. Veganism is no doubt a mysterious concept in a country that prides itself on cattle and pork. But it's not difficult to cater to a vegan; the planet is full of edible things that sprout from the earth. And yet, I was delivered a tray of bacon, sausage, scrambled eggs, yogurt and a very small bowl of fruit. The cantaloupe was dry, the strawberries too white and the green grapes bitter. The pig parts, however, looked fresh, fatty and succulent. It turned my stomach.

Finally, at exactly 9:00 am, I was retrieved by a man in his early twenties. He asked after my breakfast. I told him I was glad to be free from the smell of burnt flesh. I could tell he didn't understand the comment, but he released a genuine-sounding laugh anyway. He was an eager young staffer, perhaps an intern, who took his responsibilities very seriously. He filled our brief time together by sharing his admiration for the Trade Captain. Captain Johnson, as he called him, was not only the most intelligent person this young man had ever encountered, but he was also the most generous. He managed to perform his governmental duties while also volunteering to mentor young people like himself—allocating, as it was recounted to me, dozens of hours a week to educate and elevate the next generation of American leaders. I asked how many women Captain Johnson mentored.

The elevator door opened, and the young man passed me off to another young man without answering my question. His relief was so great that the building practically shook from his sigh.

I was left in a windowless meeting room on the fifth floor. On the walls hung four original paintings by Norman Rockwell. It was the entire Four Freedoms series. Naturally, the famous "Freedom from Want" held the most prominent place in the room. That iconic family dinner conveys an abundance everyone in America strives for, but few achieve.

I smiled as I looked at the next two paintings, equally ironic in this place. "Freedom from Fear" shows two children blissfully sleeping while their parents lovingly watch over them—the father, clutching a newspaper full of dread. America is a country run on fear. The government has its people convinced that everyone else on the planet wants what they have and will stop at nothing to get it. And yet, most in this country possess so little. Then there's "Freedom of Speech," the working class man, proudly standing amongst his peers, speaking his mind to an elevated figure out of view. Knowledge in the form of a pamphlet sprouts from his jacket pocket.

The ideas behind these images do not belong here. Even "Freedom of Worship" and its crowded pew doesn't represent what I know of America. The caption at the top "Each according to the dictates of his own conscience" has been skillfully framed out. This isn't a place where that message resonates. What I know of America is the opposite of all these things. It is a land of want, fear, repression and Christianity. So why do they hang these portraits so proudly in a windowless room very few people enter?

"Humbling, aren't they?" Trade Captain Tom Johnson said when he entered the room. "Most people find "Freedom from Want" to be their favorite, but I'm partial to the "Freedom from Fear." My kids are older now, but I still have that feeling. I still see myself standing over them, watching in loving wonder at the peacefulness of youth while dreading the state of the world."

Before I even turned to look at the Captain, I realized the uncanny likeness between the father in the painting and the man I was meeting. Suddenly, the American affection for these paintings became clear to me. It's not the ideas behind the paintings they treasure, but the actual humans they depict. The physical specimens in the paintings are what the Americans consider ideal human beings— handsome, weathered and white. A chill shot down my spine as I turned to greet my adversary.

"Trade Captain Johnson," I said, as I extended my hand.

He crossed the room in the fewest steps possible and clasped my offering with both hands. It was a firm handshake softened by the cupping of my knuckles by his left hand.

"I see your visit has caused quite a bit of unrest amongst your citizens," he said just before releasing his grip. It was a perfectly timed and respectful handshake. I've spoken with the Captain no less than a thousand times. We've been on opposite sides of a videoconference for hours on end. But we've never touched or smelled each other. There's something undeniably unique about meeting in the flesh. I became acutely aware of my other senses. It was surprising to remember that the world doesn't run on sight and sound alone.

"Yes," I replied with a subtle smile, "I had quite a welcome in San Francisco."

"I'm assuming you've heard about the rioting in New York."

"I'm afraid I haven't, no."

I kept myself composed and prepared to be inundated with insults about how wild and uncontrolled the people of the United State are. It's not something the Captain does often. But he likes to make his feelings known from time to time. I'm certain he believes that if he says it enough, I'll start to believe it. That's how the Americans are. They achieve submission through repetition. It's a civilized torture technique to which I'm quite immune.

"Well," he began, "the crowds grew so thick that people started to panic. Naturally, when you add panic to discontent, you spark rage. I understand several businesses were looted. Policemen were injured and a dozen protestors died." He paused to examine my reaction. "I'm surprised you haven't heard about this. It's all over the news."

I made the mistake of watching American news on my first trip here. I wasn't going to repeat that folly on my second. I was only ten miles past the boarder at a two-day summit in Lake Tahoe, but I may as well have been on the banks of the Mississippi. The depictions of my native country were exaggerated to the point of hilarity. The American media chastises us for our highly regulated society while simultaneously admonishing our hedonistic behavior and lack of control, and the certainty with which they report boldfaced lies is astonishing. A half hour of this manipulation and mental pretzel making was all I could take. I'm certain they find our coverage of them equally confounding. Perhaps our news organizations do focus too much on the negative aspects of their culture, but in the end, it's a false equivalency. Our news has a biased perspective, theirs is full of categorical falsehoods.

I placed my hands on the table and refocused the conversation. "I'm sure you didn't summon me here to discuss the news, Captain Johnson."

The Captain looked startled, almost offended by my sudden show of dominance.

"It really is a different experience seeing you in person," he said as he pulled a chair from the table. "Please, have a seat." He gestured, palm up, to the chair in front of me. He then sat in his wide leather seat and rolled forward until his belly was touching the light oak table.

"I am told you are not aware of the information I am about to share with you. It concerns highly classified United State information."

It was a difficult task to hide my fear, but I'm confident I did as I saw no counter reaction on the Captain's face. But his lead into the negotiation sounded more like I was about to be sabotaged. I don't have the military training to navigate such hostile behavior. My training lies in peaceful negotiation.

"And how is it that you possess this information and I do not?"

"Please allow me to finish before you ask your questions, Ms. Hope."

It was the first time he'd addressed me in that manner. It's highly unusual and mildly offensive to omit the title of a counterpart. I swallowed my reaction and gave him my full attention.

"Now," he continued, "we understand the United State's desire to move freely across the continent. How you've managed otherwise for so long is admirable. And we understand our price for this privilege has always been too high for you to consider. Surely you can understand that it would take a tremendous leap of faith on our part to allow your planes into our airspace."

"It would strictly be commercial aircraft, you know that," I interrupted.

"We are not assured by your security measures, Ms. Hope. You have difficulty controlling your people on the ground. How can you expect us to trust you'd keep fanatics out of your commercial aircrafts?"

I released an audible huff. We've had this exact conversation dozens of times and even in person, the debate felt tired and stale. Still, the fact that he led with it likely meant he'd be putting a commercial airway on the table.

"Come to your point, Trade Captain. We are both fully aware of our positions on this matter."

Once again, the Captain appeared wounded by my directness. I was behaving in the exact same manner as I always do. He'd never reacted to my style before. I couldn't help but think it was my undeniable femaleness that threw him off. On the monitor, it's easier to forget I'm a woman. A two-dimensional person can take on more of your own preferences. It's a trick of the mind to make oneself comfortable. That was not possible here. Here, he had no choice but to deal with my three-dimensional femininity. I'm proud to be a woman. That radiates.

He took a breath and dove in. "They often say that a mutual enemy is the great unifier."

"They do? Who are they?"

"Please, Ms. Hope, let me finish."

I nodded with an unavoidable smile.

"Often throughout history, two advisories have united to fight a common foe. In this instance, our common enemy is the Nation of Ute."

"The United State does not consider the Nation of Ute an enemy."

"Let me finish!" the Captain shouted. Something had him unhinged. Either that or he was truly frustrated by my behavior.

"You have something to offer us?" I asked. "Just tell me the deal and spare me the theatrics. I wasn't sent here to listen to propaganda. I was sent here to hear a deal. Let's hear it."

The Captain pushed his chair back and stood. He turned and stared at "The Freedom of Speech." After he'd summoned enough courage from the painting, he returned to the table.

"A group of programmers in Silicon Valley have hacked into the Nation of Ute's mainframe. We are told they possess the ability to shut down all launch capabilities."

"That's impossible. The Nation of Ute doesn't operate on any connected system. You can't hack into a mainframe that's not connected to anything. It is a fully self-contained system that hardly even communicates with itself. Information is moved on hard drives delivered by hand.

The only way to infiltrate their systems is to physically be there."

"I understand this. And we've never stopped trying. But as you know, the people of the Nation of Ute have used their willingness to murder millions of people to keep us on our side of the border. But this new development, I'm assured, will change all of that. Your programmers have been able to use extremely tight waveforms sent from a satellite to penetrate hard drives built before the war. As you know, that is the only technology the Nation of Ute possesses. And, as you've stated, they have to transport information from one silo to another by hand. This technology will allow you to wirelessly hack into the hardware and extract or implant information from a thousand miles away!"

The Captain was getting very excited about this technology. And I too enjoy marveling at the wonders of humanity's accomplishments. But that was not why we had been placed in this room. I had no desire to descend into the scientific nuances of a new technology. Clearly, those who understand such things have convinced our bosses of its effectiveness.

"What is the offer?" I asked.

"Ms. Hope," the Captain began, "surely you want to take a moment to rejoice with me. This is a marvelous moment. We possess the capability to neutralize the nuclear threat from the Nation of Ute."

"You mean the United State possesses the capability to neutralize the nuclear threat."

The Captain released a tremendous amount of frustration through a primal groan. "You are forgetting that this threat affects us all."

"And you are forgetting that our programmers were the ones to discover the means to neutralize it, something I'm certain America could have done had you invested more resources into your public education system. Odds that the next Einstein is born into a wealthy family capable of paying for an education in your country is remarkably low, Captain Johnson. You have to teach everyone equally or you will continue to fall behind. It baffles me how you haven't learned that lesson yet. Now, I'll ask you again, what is the offer?"

Captain Johnson pursed his lips, annoyed by my lecture, but unable to dodge the intensity of my question.

"Hand over the technology and America will grant unrestricted commercial access to our airspace."

It would be impossible to understate the enormity of the offer. It was so generous, so naked, and so completely unexpected that I found myself temporarily mute. He left almost no room for counter offers. My next logical move would have been to ask for military access to their airspace, a request that would have been unthinkable only seconds earlier. And yet, it was now the next logical step. Clearly, there was far more at stake here than a five-hour flight from New York to Los Angeles. I felt the weight of the Captain's stare.

"Well?" He asked. My mind was clouded with confusion. It was too much information to process at once.

"I'm really hungry," I said. "The only thing I could eat at breakfast was the fruit."

Captain Johnson's stare shifted to confusion.

"I'm a vegan, you know. Perhaps you can have some nuts brought in. I need some energy. I can't have this conversation without nourishment."

"We have a whole spread prepared downstairs. I just need your answer and then you can have all the nourishment you desire."

I realized then that nothing was accidental. My dossier wasn't withheld from my handlers. It was more likely studied quite closely. Everything had been designed to weaken me. The strip search conducted by a male, the excited young escort who brought me to this room, the meat-laden breakfast, and even the casual manner in which Captain Johnson addressed me. It was all highly coordinated. Captain Johnson wanted me hungry and irritated.

"So, what do you say, Ms. Hope? Do we have a deal?"

I stood up and punched my fists on the table.

"I'm not going to say another word until you bring me some nuts, Tom."

Chapter 8

Official Court Transcripts
4th Circuit Family Court, America
Pelham vs. Pelham
In the matter of custodial guardianship of five children:
Tammy Pelham, 17; Jacob Pelham, 10; Donald Pelham, 8;
Betsy Pelham, 4; and William Pelham, 2.

ATTORNEY FOR THE DEFENDANT: Ms. Pelham, please introduce yourself to the court.

NANCY PELHAM: Hello. My name is Nancy Pelham. I'm thirty-seven years old. I was born in Russellville and moved here to St. Louis when I was eighteen. I've lived here ever since.

ATTORNEY FOR THE DEFENDANT: And what is your profession, Ms. Pelham?

NANCY PELHAM: You can call me Nancy. I never cared to be called by my last name. Even young children call me Nancy. It feels more natural. Anyway, I'm a housewife, I guess. I don't know if you call that a profession, but it's what takes up most of my time. Between making meals, doing laundry, sewing costumes for Tammy's plays, shuttling the boys to their sports practices, feeding William—I'm still nursing, you know—and schooling Betsy 'cause she's too young to go just yet, I'd say my days are pretty full. I do make some time for my online course. I'm learning geological sciences. It's a real fascinating topic. I've always loved volcanoes and fault lines and things. Did you know that there are parts of the Grand Canyon where you can see the different sediment layers in the cliff? I think the place is called Parashant. Anyway, all these layers of different sediment formed different rock layers over millions of years. And when the river carved out the canyon, it left a dissection of this history for everyone to see. It's fascinating really. And I suppose if I were to have a profession, I think I'd be a geologist. Looking at million-year-old rocks strikes me as a fine way to spend a day. Am I talking too much? I'm a little nervous. This is a really important day and I just want everything to go well. But to answer your question, I don't have a profession. I just take care of the children, and John too, when we were together anyway.

ATTORNEY FOR THE DEFENDANT: Thank you Nancy. I for one believe that caring for your children is a very difficult and noble profession. Now, would you please describe for the Court your relationship with your children? And if I may, to avoid confusion, go in order of age from oldest to youngest.

NANCY PELHAM: I'd be happy to. Well, you know, Tammy and I have had our problems. Boy, I'm not gonna lie there. They say that when a girl reaches a certain age, she does not respond well to female authority. And that's certainly been the case with us. And I guess I didn't like my mama all that much when I was seventeen either. So I give her a wide berth. Let her do her thing and I try not to meddle in her affairs, you know. She's a good girl. She gets good grades, she's a wonderful actress and she's going to college next year, which I think is the most exciting thing ever. Naturally, I miss the times when we were closer, but they'll come around again, I just know it. And I got to spend lots of great time with her when she was young, you know, 'cause the boys didn't come around until she was seven.

Speaking of the boys, well they're just so delightful. Jacob is whip-smart for a ten-year-old. He's good at sports, sure, but I've never seen a child tackle a math problem as fast as this boy. He's doing algebra for crying out loud. I didn't even know what algebra was until I was… well, I still probably couldn't define it for you, so please don't ask. Point is, the child is smart, athletic, and the sweetest thing on two legs. I'm sorry he's not gonna get to play wide receiver on account of his eyes. But, the Lord gives us what He thinks we can handle, and I'm sure Jacob will make due… Oh, I'm getting some funny looks from you all. I'm sorry, I forgot John didn't tell you about that. You'd think he'd know. Jacob has an inoperable corneal anomaly in his left eye. Well, it's operable, but the operation would really be an extraction; so, we've chosen not to operate. Anyway, he can see just fine doing normal things, but tracking a football against the blue sky, well, that's not something his eyes will let him do. There are other pursuits in this world and I'm sure he'll find one he enjoys just as much.

Now, Donald, sweet little Donald. I'm watching him. I'm not sure what kind of man he's going to grow into. He's very observant, very outspoken, and very sensitive. And I'd say that's about the worst combination of attributes a person can have. If you notice everything and then say something about all those things you noticed, then cry when anyone questions what you noticed, life is gonna get real hard. And I know he can't help any one of these things. His daddy just tries to get him to stop crying. Me, I'm trying to get him to stop talking, when in reality, we all should be encouraging him to stop noticing what other people got to say about his noticing. That way, he can still be observant, outspoken and sensitive. The world needs more sensitive boys, don't you think?

Betsy, I'm gonna be honest with ya'll right now; Betsy is probably gonna be the death of me. She's super bright for a four-year-old. And right now, her and I get along famously. She doesn't cry or cause any kind of trouble. She's the most obedient of all my children, so I'm always letting her play by herself and do what she wants. But I just know, when she gets to be Tammy's age, her and I are gonna fight something fierce. And she does weird things in her bedroom that I'm not sure I like. I asked her once why she spread out all them little squares of fabric and was stirring the laundry in the hamper. She told me she was making a witch's brew and that those pieces of fabric were the frogs she'd cut open so their insides would dry out so she could make a powder. Have you ever heard of such a thing? I talked to our pastor about it. I told him I thought Betsy was getting involved with the Occult, that somehow, the devil was talking to her, telling her to disembowel imaginary frogs and cook up witch potions. He said that she just had an active imagination and that I shouldn't worry about it unless she starts using real frogs. But I wondered, she's not even in school yet, where would she ever get the idea to do such things. That's when my friend Dorothy told me, and I believe this to be true, once you have one kid in school, they're all exposed. Children transmit information just as surely as they do germs.

Finally, we have William. Strong little William. I put him down and he takes off like a bowling ball-sized rodent. He'll smash into anything and keep on going. I swear to you I didn't mean it, but I dropped him down the stairs once, and the boy just got up and kept on crawling, didn't cry or nothing… oh dear, I probably shouldn't have said that. It was an accident, Judge, it coulda happened to anyone.

ATTORNEY FOR THE DEFENDANT: That's quite alright, Nancy. I think everyone here understands how squirmy little boys can be. Now, would you please tell the court how you plan on caring for your children should you be granted custody.

NANCY PELHAM: Well, I suppose I would just keep doing what I'm doing. I think I've done a pretty good job so far and the kids seem happy.

ATTORNEY FOR THE DEFENDANT: Well yes, there's no doubt you'd take great care of these children. What I'm asking is, how will you pay for it?

NANCY PELHAM: Oh! Well of course. I expect that John will contribute most of the money for the house and basics. That is, I presume, why he wants custody, so he won't have to give me any money. But you know, the church has also said they'd help out with some of the basics. They do a food drive twice a year and collect a basement full of canned and dry goods. It's meant for families in need, and the preacher said that if I got custody of my kids and I needed anything, why, I would qualify just as sure as anyone. It's not the best situation, but it's something. I can't really go to work just yet, not with Betsy and William so young. So I'm afraid my options are limited.

ATTORNEY FOR THE DEFENDANT: But you have a strong support system, correct?

NANCY PELHAM: Indeed I do. I have the best support system a woman could ask for. I have all my friends at the church. And I consider practically everyone in the congregation my friend. And then there's all the parents at the school too—Jacob and Donald's school. The parents and the staff are all real kind and want to see me continue to be an active part in my children's lives and the school for that matter. It's all connected, you know, the communities. We're all connected. John isn't connected to the community like I am. He's got his own thing going on with his work friends and that's alright, I guess. But he's not a part of the community like I am. The community really supports me. And that's what I want for my children. I want them to be accepted, supported and loved by their community. After all, that's all anyone can ask for, right? Besides health and peace, that is. Being a part of a community makes us better people.

ATTORNEY FOR THE DEFENDANT: I couldn't agree with you more. Community provides the bedrock for a healthy society and healthy individuals. Thank you so much, Ms. Pelham, for your thoughtful and honest answers. You may step down.

Chapter 9

An open letter to a future generation
Nation of Ute

It is very important for future generations to understand that the Nation of Ute didn't act capriciously. Sacrificing so many souls for the mere possibility of peace was not something we took lightly. But the civil war was only intensifying, and as the divide between the two factions grew deeper, so did the violence. If we hadn't acted when we did, those people wouldn't have the ability to share the continent the way they do now, divided or not. They quite simply would have kept fighting until there was nothing left of the other side. And that, according to the Nation of Ute, would have been a defeat for everyone.

The official beginning of the war, if we are to assert there be one, was when the military, built up over centuries by the Old Country, disbanded. Militias had long been formed, but they were largely kept in check by the more heavily armed military, a military that acted on the authority of one government. But once the Old Country's federal government collapsed, all four branches of their fighting services disappeared overnight. The militias were then free to do as they saw fit.

Military bases were extremely beneficial resources to the side that occupied them. But these resources were not evenly distributed between the United State and America, at least not according to the new battle lines. And while the territories controlled by the United State occupied the entire west coast as well as the coastal Northeast, America controlled a much larger land mass, and as such, a larger share of the military institutions.

Once the command structure dissolved, military personnel became free to do as they pleased. Many soldiers joined their families and enrolled with their local militias. Others formed small military groups to support the side of their allegiance. When it came to troop numbers, the advantage was America's. The military industrial complex had always attracted a more conservative individual, and America was the more conservative country. Plus, once in the military, you were trained to follow orders without question. So, when soldiers had the opportunity to choose a side, the authoritarian style of America was a more natural fit.

In the end, however, it wasn't the number of soldiers supporting the militias that mattered. It was the equipment; and the moment the dissolution of the military was announced, the borders between the warring sides were drawn. And, like the bases, whatever equipment existed on each side was there to stay. Soldiers moved quickly, but the physical resources were geo-locked.

So the war had officially started and the new boarders were drawn artificially along old state lines. This triggered the fastest and largest migration of humans in history. In less than a week, forty million people moved between the two new territories. Families were torn apart and others were reunited. Schools and community centers overflowed with refugees from the other side until eventually, people began squatting in abandoned homes, seizing the property. It was as if the entire Old Country were engaged in a massive game of musical chairs. In the end, what America had in land, the United State possessed in people. By the time the ramparts were raised along the official boarders, sixty-three percent of the Old Country had chosen to live in the more progressive land which had been labeled the United State.

At first, each side employed as much of their military might as possible. Air raids over population centers were performed on a regular basis, but coordinating these attacks became increasingly difficult without the unified support of ground crew, air traffic control, and maintenance teams. The old military was a well-oiled machine that relied on teams built from individuals with specialized training. Even one missing skill could ground a mission. So, after a month of watching the skies, the battles refocused on the ground. After all, it was land they were fighting over now, plain and simple.

America's territorial dominance was profound. The United State was a nation united by ideology but divided by geography. They had to stay laser focused simply to maintain a cohesive front. America repeatedly tried to capitalize on this physical division by pitting one coast against the other, but their attempts to divide the enemy were not successful.

It wasn't easy for America to defend two fronts with a population that had declined so significantly during the migration. Every able-bodied male was expected to report to either the western or northeastern fronts. The center of the country became a protected convalescent center for women, children, and the elderly. If the United State breached the border, passing through the line of heavily-armed men, they could travel into a largely open land with little resistance. But that rarely happened. The Americans were ruthless in defending their land. Their excessive weaponry and willingness to use it freely made their borders extremely secure.

The physical battles continued for months on end. One side would push the border ten miles in one direction only to have the other side—twenty miles down the border—push it ten miles back. The battle lines moved like a serpent, keeping everyone along the borders in a constant state of confusion and unease. There were breaches in security allowing rogue teams behind enemy lines, and they'd manage to terrorize a community for a day or two. But nobody over the age of ten was without a gun, so any small operation behind enemy lines was quickly snuffed.

Historically speaking, the largest toll the war took on the people of the Old Country didn't come from the bullets being fired over the ramparts. It was the battle that started long before people took up arms. It was the psychological cyber-battle. The battle of hatred waged through technology. That battle killed the souls of the living—present and future.

Each country was well guarded from cyber-attacks. The Old Country's technological tussles with Russia had spurned tremendous advancements in cyber-security and offline sharing of information via small chips became commonplace. This was a benefit each side enjoyed. But just as before, there was a public interface where the warring countries could communicate with each other. And in this forum, well-chosen words, images and videos became powerful and exacting weapons available to almost everyone. This battle of the minds was unlike anything humanity had ever seen. And it involved the entire population. This vile exchange of violent thoughts and ideas entrenched each side deeper into the ground than would befit a corpse, burying any chance of resurrection.

Chapter 10

Debriefing Notes
North American Trade Summit
Jackie Hope, Chief Minister of Trade for the United State

The nuts arrived in less than two minutes. But those were two very long minutes. The Captain's breathing was unnaturally loud for a man of his size. It was like sharing a stable with a racehorse after three turns around the track.

Once the bowl was placed before me and the young man who'd delivered them was on the other side of the door, I scooped up a handful of the salted mixture. Peanuts, cashews and almonds combined their subtle flavors on my tongue. I chewed slowly, thinking through the situation. What was the wisdom in sharing this breakthrough with the Americans? Why wouldn't we just de-activate the missiles ourselves? And why were the Americans willing to give up so much for the privilege of doing it? Why wouldn't they simply allow us to perform the task? My stomach settled after my third portion of nuts. And thankfully, my mind began to clear.

"Now, Chief Minister, you've had your nuts. I'm told you've been granted the full authority of your government to make this decision alone. And, you are not to leave this room until you do. So, I respectfully request your answer."

The Captain's disposition had returned to the more formal man I'd come to know over videoconference. The change was so dramatic that the room suddenly took on a two-dimensional feel, as though we'd transformed into wallpaper or better yet, the characters in the Norman Rockwell paintings that surrounded us.

"Now that we have this technology, why is it so important that America be the one to disarm the Nation of Ute?"

"Because your government has said they will not."

It was odd that he knew more about my government's positions than I did. But the answer rang true. Nobody wants nuclear weapons pointed at them. But so long as they were, the United State could be assured that America wouldn't attack.

"Let me ask you, Trade Captain Johnson, what do you suppose are the other applications of this technology? Certainly neutralizing the nuclear missiles in the Nation of Ute is a noble achievement, one that would be of great benefit to both our countries. But there must be something more here. There must be a reason your initial offer—and I am taking that as an *initial* offer—was so generous. What does this technology offer that you'd be willing to allow the United State unrestricted access to American airspace?"

Captain Johnson released an uncomfortable laugh. "I said unrestricted *commercial* access."

"And I said unrestricted access," I replied. This was how the conversation would naturally progress. We've performed these bargaining dances so many times. I'm embarrassed to admit that we've yet to set even one deal. But this was unlike any of our other attempts. I realized that when I saw how my counter landed on the Captain's face. He continued to display an unusual amount of unease.

"I'm not authorized to grant military access," he said. "You may have unrestricted commercial access. That is our final offer."

"What about our weak security? Aren't you afraid terrorists might get on our commercial flights and wreak havoc over the skies of America?"

"We'd have joint security personnel at all airports with flights over America."

I'm sorry to report that I was not able to maintain my composure. I burst into a loud and ugly laugh, shooting several nut particles across the table.

"There is no way we're allowing your Gestapo Goons to frisk our people. Especially when they're traveling within their own country."

"But they're traveling over ours."

"No. Absolutely not."

"I thought we were negotiating here, Chief Minister. There must be some give and take."

"You just put a condition on your initial offer."

"That was always a condition of my initial offer."

"Then why didn't you say so from the start? I wouldn't have had a mouthful of nuts then."

"Consider the benefits…"

"It's not going to happen, Trade Captain. Unless you're planning an invasion, your soldiers will never set foot on our soil."

"Let's not be dramatic, Minister Hope. Think of the benefits a deal like this could spawn. Haven't we always said that the first deal was going to be the hardest? You know that once we break the ice, the water will flow freely. Imagine what a deal like this could grow into? If our people interact with your people on a regular basis, we can begin to break down stereotypes and misconceptions. That kind of constant interaction can only do good for our relations."

"You're misrepresenting the relationship here, Trade Captain. Your people would be interrogating my people. They are allowed to travel freely in their own country and will not endure your security practices. Please don't insult me with your distortions of the truth. I'm not one of your brainwashed sheep you call citizens. I see quite clearly what's before me."

"Now who's insulting whom, Trade Minister?"

"Oh, lay off the act, Captain. Don't pretend you're offended. You've been calling my people wild monkeys for years. The amendment to your initial offer is categorically rejected. If that is a deal breaker for you, then I suppose we're done here."

The Captain walked around the room surveying the paintings. It appeared as though he was deciding which depiction of the human experience would give him the inspiration he was seeking. I expected him to land on "Freedom of Worship." I'd given him so little space to move, prayer was the logical next step for an American. But instead, he landed on "Freedom from Fear." He reached up with his right hand and caressed the head of the sleeping boy. I cringed at the touch. Human oils do not blend well with the oils of our images. Our chemistry supports life, not the life-like. I feared for the integrity of that imaginary boy's shape.

"I want to protect my people, Trade Minister Hope. I want them to feel safe. That's something I don't think you've ever been able to understand about me. Sure, I want my people to prosper too. I want them to enjoy their lives as I'm sure you do. But they can't do that unless they feel safe. And their safety is my primary concern. Everything else is secondary. If my people don't feel safe, they cannot enjoy any of the other fruits of life. And security is the best defense against fear. You must understand, Trade Minister, I can't have my people forced underground. We need to feel safe to walk in the sunshine. I implore you to reconsider your position. Share with us your technology so we can put an end to this constant fear and we will grant you the sky."

It was the most sincere and impassioned pitch I'd ever heard from the Trade Captain. And I will admit, I was impressed with his poetic finish, but not nearly enough to subject my people to the whims of American soldiers.

"Unrestricted airspace, no joint security," I said.

The Captain shook his head. "I've already told you, I'm not authorized to allow military access."

"Then what are you authorized to allow?" I asked. Surely there was something more the Captain could give. He was an expert negotiator. He wouldn't put everything on the table right away.

"The western slope," he stated with resignation.

"I'm sorry?"

"I'm authorized to offer you the western slope."

"I'm afraid I don't know what that is."

"The western slope of the Nation of Ute. I'm offering you the western half of the Nation of Ute."

"You don't control the Nation of Ute. It's not yours to offer."

The Captain stood in silence and allowed me to catch up. I scooped up another fistful of nuts and chewed them slowly. I wondered, were they planning on invading the moment the missiles were compromised? Would it be a sneak attack or would they drop leaflets announcing the invasion? Would there be summits and conferences brokering a peaceful transition? Then my mind refocused from an imagined future to the very real and recent past. How long have they known about our technology? How long have we had it? The Americans certainly appeared to have had time to plan for this meeting, which meant my own government had thought this through as well. They too must have a plan. So why did they send me? Why put me in a room blind with people who can clearly see the stakes? On the surface, it appeared to be a recipe for disaster. A suicide mission. Unless... That's when I realized for the second time that day that nothing had been left to chance. Like the Americans, my own government knew me well. They didn't send me here to parse apart the Nation of Ute. The President knows I'm a Ute sympathizer. She wouldn't ever put me in a position where I could be implicated in their demise. If we truly did have this technology, using it or sharing it would produce the same result. Either way, the Americans would be free to pursue war.

My decision was clear. Only one question remained. Why was I sent to make a decision of unquantifiable magnitude and given so little information?

I looked across the table at the Captain. I could tell he desperately wanted to complete this negotiation. His anxiety bubbled deep inside his chest, which affected his breathing. He'd learn soon enough that this meeting was merely another scene in the epic play between our two nations. Only now the power had shifted quite dramatically into our hands. The lights were about to come up on this new act; I had to play my part.

"Why do you suppose I was sent here without first being briefed on the nature of this technology?"

"As you know," the Trade Captain began, "trust between our two countries comes with great labor, if at all. Your president sent you here blind as a gesture of sincerity, as though it were something tangible—a blanket to make us feel secure in your decision."

I marveled for a moment at the tremendous faith placed upon me by my superiors. Then I realized they weren't being genuine at all. Sending me blind to make this decision in such a short time demonstrates the ridiculousness of America's request for our technology and highlights the power we now possess over them. I wasn't sent here to negotiate. I was sent to rub their noses in our newfound power.

"I'm sorry, Trade Captain Johnson," I said. "It is clear to me what decision I must make and I'm afraid I cannot accept your terms. Additionally, the United State will not share this new technology with America. Not now and not ever. Nor will we share with America our decision to use it."

He was crestfallen. It was as though I'd stabbed his children before his very eyes. It was not the reaction I was expecting. It was far too dramatic and emotional. I continued.

"I thank you for your time and hospitality. You'll forgive me but my duty demands I leave immediately. I apologize that I will not be able to join you for lunch."

He didn't say another word. He just turned and continued staring at the sleeping children in the painting, his shoulders falling toward his knees.

"Good day, Trade Captain Johnson."

Chapter 11

Official Court Transcripts
4th Circuit Family Court, America
Pelham vs. Pelham
In the matter of custodial guardianship of five children:
Tammy Pelham, 17; Jacob Pelham, 10; Donald Pelham, 8;
Betsy Pelham, 4; and William Pelham, 2.

ATTORNEY FOR THE PLAINTIFF: Thank you Ms. Pelham. We all appreciate your testimony. And I think I speak for the entire court when I say that being a housewife is indeed a career. Perhaps the most difficult of all.

NANCY PELHAM: Well, it's a lot of work for sure. But it's also my duty as a mother, you know. It's the responsibility you assume when you have children. So, it's a job yes. But I don't know, a career makes it all sound so cold and calculated. It's not like a job that you get up and go to day after day. I don't think of it like that. I like to think of it as being a mother.

ATTORNEY FOR THE PLAINTIFF: A housewife.

NANCY PELHAM: Yes.

ATTORNEY FOR THE PLAINTIFF: Only you're not a wife anymore, are you? You stopped being a wife when you decided to break your solemn vows and leave your husband. So we can't really call you a housewife, can we? Now you're better described as a housekeeper, isn't that right?

NANCY PELHAM: That's ridiculous. I'm so much more than that Russian prostitute John wants to hire. I'm their mother, for Pete's sake. I gave birth to them. They share my eye color, my hair, my tissue paper skin that sunburns in minutes. Sure, I'm not a wife any more. I stopped being a wife when my husband broke our bond and started sleeping with other women. But I'm still bonded to my children.

ATTORNEY FOR THE PLAINTIFF: Yes, you are. And you had a lot to say about that special bond between a mother and her daughter in your earlier testimony. You and your eldest daughter aren't on the best of terms, and you have all but assured us that you'll have a terrible relationship with your youngest, when she comes of age. So I'm curious, Ms. Pelham, can you tell us about your relationship with your own mother?

NANCY PELHAM: Well now, I don't think you're being very fair. I never said I was gonna have a terrible relationship with Betsy. That's not what I said at all. And I know Tammy and I will see eye to eye again real soon. She just needs her space is all. When she comes to visit from college, she'll be a different lady, I just know it.

ATTORNEY FOR THE PLAINTIFF: Please just answer the questions as I ask them, Ms. Pelham. I'd like to hear about your relationship with your mother.

NANCY PELHAM: What does that have to do with my children?

ATTORNEY FOR THE PLAINTIFF: Is it true that you ran away from home?

NANCY PELHAM: Well, I... I did. And if you must know, my momma and I don't talk. Haven't talked in over twenty years now.

ATTORNEY FOR THE PLAINTIFF: Ever since you ran away to St. Louis. And why don't you and your mother talk? She's still alive, you know. Your dad is too. I called them down in Russellville. They're both very healthy, if you care to know.

NANCY PELHAM: Well, I guess you already know everything then, don't you?

ATTORNEY FOR THE PLAINTIFF: Yes, but we'd like to hear it from you. Why did you leave home, Ms. Pelham? And why don't you talk to your parents anymore?

NANCY PELHAM: This was all so long ago. But I'll tell you if you want. I was seeing a boy. Been seeing him since I was fifteen. Momma and daddy didn't approve on account that he was twenty-three when we met. I fell in love. It was foolish, I know that now, but I was head over heels for that boy. My parents did everything they could to keep me from him. But I was determined to spend the rest of my life with that man. Well, when I got to be old enough and finished my schooling, I decided I was going to leave Russellville and move to St. Louis with this boy. He was twenty-six by that time and I was just eighteen. When I told my parents, we had a terrible fight. I'll admit, I said some very awful things. And when my daddy hit me across the face, the pain was bad. But when my momma told him to do it again, I swore on my grandma's grave I would never say another word to either of them ever again. And so I haven't. I'm a woman of my word, counselor. I have integrity. Ain't nobody can accuse me otherwise.

ATTORNEY FOR THE PLAINTIFF: And what happened then?

NANCY PELHAM: Well, a week after I moved to St. Louis with my boyfriend, he left me for another woman. An older, more sophisticated woman. That was when I met John.

ATTORNEY FOR THE PLAINTIFF: Yes, you met your ex-husband that very day, correct? The same day your old boyfriend dumped you?

NANCY PELHAM: Yes. We met at a bar.

ATTORNEY FOR THE PLAINTIFF: Indeed. A bar where men go to proposition women. Correct? Are you familiar with the saying, "Those who live in glass houses shouldn't throw stones?"

NANCY PELHAM: If you're insinuating that I prostituted myself, you're dead wrong. I've never been paid for sexual relations. Never. I had no money, counselor. No money and nowhere to go. I just went there for... I was scared and alone.

ATTORNEY FOR THE PLAINTIFF: But you did sleep with John Pelham that very night, did you not?

NANCY PELHAM: Is that against the law? We were young. Very, very young. I didn't know that was a place where amorous boys went. I don't see what any of this has to do with my children. We went through all of this during the divorce.

ATTORNEY FOR THE PLAINTIFF: You said you were scared and alone and that you had no money. What's going to happen when the church food doesn't come? Or when John's money isn't enough? What are you going to do then?

NANCY PELHAM: I'll find a way. I'm very resourceful.

ATTORNEY FOR THE PLAINTIFF: Yes, you are. You were resourceful enough to find a new man the very day you lost your old one. Tell us, Mrs. Pelham, are you currently in a relationship?

NANCY PELHAM: No.

ATTORNEY FOR THE PLAINTIFF: Have you had relations with anyone other than your husband?

NANCY PELHAM: I did. I was involved with a man for a brief time after John and I separated. It was a difficult time. I was hurting and I needed someone to talk to. Someone to comfort me. It was too soon after our marriage. I acknowledged that and broke it off.

ATTORNEY FOR THE PLAINTIFF: Or, did you break if off because you didn't want it to affect this trial? And didn't you start seeing this man before you got your divorce?

NANCY PELHAM: We broke it off. It was a mistake and it's over.

ATTORNEY FOR THE PLAINTIFF: But don't you see the pattern here? Every time you're scared and alone, you find yourself in bed with a man you've only just met. Perhaps, Ms. Pelham, you should have listened to your mother. Perhaps you should be spending less time in the sack with random men. Perhaps you should be giving less "space" to your eldest daughter, who right this very minute could be making the same mistakes as you. Please tell me again how this has nothing to do with your children. Your behavior, Ms. Pelham, has everything to do with your children.

NANCY PELHAM: I am a good woman and an excellent mother. I'm not proud of everything I've done, but I have only ever done what's best for my children and nothing more. How dare you accuse me of being a loose, inattentive mother! I'm the exact opposite of what you're describing. I started seeing Thomas because I needed comfort. I was scared. ~~John was getting drunk and hitting me~~.

ATTORNEY FOR THE PLAINTIFF: Ms. Pelham, that evidence has been sealed by the previous judge. You were specifically instructed not to bring it up. Not here, not anywhere. Judge, you are obligated to disregard the defendant's last statement. Reporter, please strike the defendant's last statement from the transcripts.

NANCY PELHAM: I am not going to let that man hit my children!

ATTORNEY FOR THE PLAINTIFF: Has your husband ever hit any of your children? Think before you answer, Ms. Pelham. You are under oath. Are you aware of your husband ever hitting any of your children?

NANCY PELHAM: No. No, he hasn't. ~~But he hit me! He'd taken to hitting me quite often before I left him. That's why I left and that's why I don't want him to have custody of my children.~~

ATTORNEY OF THE PLAINTIFF: Judge, once again I ask that you disregard the defendant's last three statements and that they be stricken from the record. Ms. Pelham, the truth is, your ex-husband has been nothing but good to you. He's provided for you and your children. He shouldn't have to support you just because you've decided to move on to yet another man. I have no further questions.

Chapter 12

Before the official beginning of the war—when the government of the Old Country was still functioning—there was a hope that the institutions we'd built up would protect us from each other. There's an important distinction to note here, one that illustrates how deep the animosity had already gotten. Had the people hoped the institutions would protect us from *ourselves*, we may have avoided the war. But, by then, the unity of the Old Country had died and people were looking to the institutions as a defense against the other side.

Now, without getting into the hot debate about who actually started the war, I will tell you it was the people of the West Coast who pulled away first. Their actions were quickly followed by the Northeast. These regions used their local governments to enact laws that were in direct opposition to the laws that were being passed in the nation's capital. It was—they wrote in each new law—the only way they could protect their people.

Most of these laws pertained to the funding of education, the protection of the environment, access to affordable healthcare and the treatment and processing of immigrants both lawful and unlawful, as well as the defense of basic civil liberties. These issues had long been a source of great debate in the Old Country but never to the point where one side would secede. It wasn't until the federal government began passing laws on who could vote that it became necessary for localities to take drastic measures. The people of the Old Country were willing to accept that a majority sometimes wanted things a certain way and voted accordingly. But when it became apparent that the government was fixing the electorate to ensure a specific direction regardless of the majority, the people did the only thing they could and took a stand locally.

This was the civil beginning to the Second Civil War.

Part of the national problem was that there had been a strong and sustained movement toward the smallest government possible. Theory was that a small government meant less interference into the lives of its citizens. But as this movement began to achieve its goals, it became evident to anyone paying attention that the smaller the government was, the less democratic it became. It didn't take long before a series of autocrats had assumed control and surrounded themselves with spineless yes men whose sole purpose was to maintain the image of democratic representation. Many will say these leaders were the cancer of the Old Country, but they were merely a symptom. The cancer was already embedded in the society.

Once the autocrats had firm control, they began passing their laws; laws that gave more freedom to industry and less to the people. They managed to turn a traditional conservatism on its head by exacting more governmental control over the people, not less. They mandated a national registry based on race and political affiliations. They withheld public assistance until certain tests were passed. They criminalized protest. They assumed control over the media. And most notably, they instituted polling requirements. A test to ensure your fitness to vote was now required before being granted the privilege to do so. The country then moved swiftly into this very dark time. All the while, the supporters of this government loudly cheered their leader's progress while the coastal resistance dutifully organized.

The battles between federal and local law waged in the courtrooms while the struggles for free speech, fair and open elections, and the right to publicly assemble were waged in the streets. Local police, whose orders and funding came from the municipalities, protected the mostly peaceful protestors from the increasing threat of federal intervention. And we moved closer to war.

The unofficial start of the Second Civil War was the Labor Day Lock Out.

In the Old Country, the first Monday of September was a holiday called Labor Day. This was a day to celebrate and recognize the people and laws of the Labor Movement, a movement that led to the greatest era of prosperity the Old Country would ever see. Through the combination of collective bargaining, fair wages, and governmental oversight, industry grew, and a large segment of the population profited. The era was short-lived, and an unchecked capitalism quickly eroded labor policies in favor of marketplace governance.

The Labor Day Lockout was a simple and extremely effective protest against the federal government. On that day, the West Coast stopped all shipments of goods to the rest of the country. Everything they produced as well as all the imports shipped through their ports no longer traveled more than 300 miles from the coast. Arrangements were made to move goods across Canada to the Northeast. But the rest of the Old Country was left without.

There wasn't immediate alarm. The lockout appeared to be nothing more than a shipping disruption, something everyone had experienced at one time or another. But as the weeks wore on, the shelves of the resistance bent with abundance, while the rest of the country began to live without.

At first, the people complained about not receiving their Chinese trinkets and other cheap goods produced overseas. But soon they realized that the Labor Day Lockout had a far more profound consequence—food. Over 60% of all fruits and vegetables consumed in the Old Country came from the West Coast. One-third of the dairy and 95% of the nuts were also produced there. Prices skyrocketed in the boycotted areas as availability plummeted. It was a dramatic move, but the resistance was desperate. It appeared as though the only way they could get the government's attention was to starve half its people.

On the seventh week of the lockout, the federal government sent the National Guard to collect and ship produce. Only, once they started doing that, the farmers refused to produce. The government was then left with no other choice. They sent the Army in to seize the land. The resistance, understanding they were outgunned, physically occupied the space in such numbers that it became impossible to remove them all without slaughtering them.

This demonstration of aggression by the government forced the resistance to organize even further. And they did so with their second greatest resource, money. The coastal factions dissolved their former state lines and began calling themselves the United State, a nod to the Old Country but with a defiant singularity. They were quick to discontinue all funding of the federal government and began moving their incredible financial resources into separate secured accounts. Now, not only did the United State control a majority of the food, they also possessed a majority of the Old Country's financial assets.

This event was once again met by military action. Battleships were sent to New York harbor as a warning. They sailed in with cannons up as if they were about to perform a smash and grab bank robbery on the entire city. The people of the United State responded by lining the shores—one hundred deep—and stared down the approaching soldiers. Once again, America's choice was to retreat or conduct a massacre on a frightening scale. The ships were forced to sail away.

Despite the unrest and the glaringly obvious national division, the government remained steadfast in its conviction to reunite the country by forcing the United State into submission. But with an ever-shrinking food supply and a rapidly dwindling financial coffer, they had no choice but to seek assistance overseas.

There had been episodes of violence all along this slog toward war. It wasn't unusual for riots to flare up and die down in every part of the Old Country. But when it was

confirmed that the autocratic efforts of the federal government of the United States of America was being financially supported by Russia, the violence exploded with a decisive speed and an explosive force. Two months later, the government failed, the military dissolved,
and the war officially began.

Chapter 13

My journey from Houston to Cuba was unpleasant for a number of reasons, not the least of which was the terrible ocean conditions. Throughout the tumultuous journey, I continued to assure myself that I'd performed my duty exactly as intended. And yet, the unusual nature of the Trade Captain's response had me perplexed. The utter defeat that washed over his body as I left the room was haunting. Was I wrong to believe that this was merely an opening salvo and that we'd be barking at each other through our screens the moment I returned to the United State?

   I checked into my hotel and immediately headed to the beach. There, on the crowded sandy shore, looking out over the vast Caribbean, I could focus my thoughts. Cuba has always been a very special place. The culture, the food and the people are as inviting as they are interesting. But since the end of the war, it's taken on an additional uniqueness. This is a land where citizens of a certain mind from the United State and America can be together peacefully. Its popularity as a vacation destination in both countries is unmatched, which is why the Cubans do not tolerate violence or aggression of any kind, anywhere on their island. There is too much money to be made by not taking sides and keeping the peace.

It is hard to tell, looking out over the crowded beach, who is from the US and who is from America. They are only people. Overweight, underweight, young and old. They all perform the same generic vacation tasks to help them relax. Sleep in the sun. Swim in the ocean. Read a good book. And have a good laugh. Naturally, there is very little interaction between our people, but they are on the same beach and in the same water, and that must count for something.

I sat on that beach for hours watching families come and go. The weather was perfect and the sea had calmed. The light, the activity around me, and my own wondering mind had put me in a sort of trance. My unfocused gaze fell onto a woman handing a data card to her friend. The exchange was quick and unremarkable. The data was most likely a film or music they were sharing. A similar exchange probably took place hundreds of times on that beach that very afternoon. But when I saw it, I looked up into the light blue sky. Somewhere up there was a satellite, probably many, which would eventually have the ability to extract all the information on that data card, or worse, implant a virus to corrupt the next machine it goes into.

That was when I remembered what Trade Captain Johnson said. He'd said he couldn't have his people forced underground. They needed to be able to walk in the sunshine. He wasn't talking about sheltering people from nuclear war. He was talking about the eventuality that the United State would improve upon this breakthrough and be able to hack into modern machines. And once that happened, all their technology would need to move underground.

I would share this fear if I didn't have absolute faith in the integrity of my government. We wouldn't risk destabilizing the peace by engaging in hostile espionage. Sure, there is plenty of spying and reconnaissance happening on both sides, but to engage in such brazen activity would surely be considered an act of aggression, an act that would be met by an unthinkable consequence. The United State's interests lie in maintaining the status quo.

Perhaps I have too much faith in my country. But remember, it is my duty to hold the torch of optimism so we can forge through this dark time. And at that moment, I was overwhelmed by the desire to share that light.

I ran to my room, leaving all my valuables on the beach, an error I was certain would be met with disappointment upon my return. I called guest services and requested a secure line to America. I got through to the Trade Department much quicker than I was used to. When I made this exact same call from the United State, I could be on hold for over forty minutes. Here in Cuba, I was patched through in less than three.

I spoke the moment an attendant appeared on the screen.

"I'd like to speak with Trade Captain Johnson please. This is the United State Chief Minister of Trade calling from Cuba. Please tell him it's very important."

The attendant was a boy who looked and sounded exactly like the young man who'd escorted me to my meeting. Surely it wasn't the same boy. But theirs is a breeding ground of homogeny on so many uncomfortable levels.

"Chief Minister," the Trade Captain said cheerfully as he slid into view. He was out of breath and excited, as though he'd ran to take the call.

"Trade Captain, I hope I'm not disturbing you."

"No, not at all. Have you reconsidered your position?"

"No. I'm afraid I have not."

His cheer vanished with blinding speed. The switch of a button would have been slower.

"Is everything alright?" I asked, sensing—once again—his unusual dread.

"Chief Minister," Captain Johnson said with a sigh, "why have you called?"

"Well, I wanted to share with you something you may not understand about my people and my government."

The Trade Captain looked to someone off screen, then appeared to send them out of the room.

"I realize now that I wasn't being very sensitive when we met. I needed some time to process what you'd told me and well… I don't want you to fear for your children. I don't want anyone in America to live in fear. The freedom from fear is what makes living in the United State so special. Sure, we have our problems, and yes, there is danger and violence. But that exists everywhere. That's life. It's only when we allow it to control how we live that we become shackled. We are not going to use this technology against the Nation of Ute, and we're certainly not going to use it against you. You have my word on that. I know I'm not the president, but she works for me, me and the millions of other people who elected her. And we're not going to put innocent lives on the line for the privilege of spying on you. I want you and your children to live with the freedom to speak and worship. I want for you and yours to live free of want, and most importantly, free from fear. So while I know we cannot make a deal at this time, I wanted you to hear me say that. Even if you don't believe me, I thought you should hear it."

The Trade Captain was silent for a moment. I couldn't be sure, but it appeared as though tears were forming in his eyes.

"Thank you, Chief Minister. Your sentiments are comforting. And I believe you. Despite all my training that says I shouldn't, I believe you. And it is also my wish that we live in peace. But we do not live in a world built on wishes. We live in a world built on fear. And my government is afraid that no matter how sincere your overtures are to the contrary, one way or another, you'll use this technology to destroy us."

"We won't. I'll have my president on the phone with yours in an hour. They can discuss this. You and I can steer them in the right direction. We've done it before."

"Those were very small disputes we resolved, Chief Minister. This is beyond our capacity to assist. I'm afraid it's already too late."

"Too late? What do you mean by too late? It's not too late. We've only just begun talking about this."

The Trade Captain inhaled deeply, calming the erratic breathing that had been plaguing him.

"In less than one hour, America will launch seven missiles aimed at United State Satellites."

"What are you saying?"

"We cannot allow your country the unchecked ability to spy on us. We will not allow it. By removing the satellites, we will at least buy ourselves enough time to secure our technology belowground."

"But that would constitute an act of aggression, Tom. The consequences of such an act are shared by both our people. You can't do this."

"I'm afraid it's already done. I'm sorry, Jackie. I truly am. I wish we lived in a more trusting world. I wish we didn't have to hate each other so much."

"We don't, Tom."

There was a long pause.

"Hold your little girls tight when you see them," Tom said, his voice slipping toward silence. "I wish we could leave them a better world," he exclaimed before shuttering the communication.

"We can, Tom," I said to the darkened monitor, unable to accept the fact that I was now alone. "But we have to make it that way through trust. We have to trust each other. Even if we don't like each other, we have to trust each other."

I walked in a daze back onto the beach. The families were still blissfully enjoying their vacations; my valuables were untouched. Soon the mood would change. Once the news came, it would be impossible to ignore. I was rapidly falling into a state of depression when I remembered something else the Trade Captain had said. He'd said that throughout history, adversaries have united against a common foe. I've always found that to be an excuse for the adversaries to be lazy and not look inward and work on their own disagreements. But then, as I imagined the scene soon to unfold on this integrated island, I realized the truth in that statement.

Once we learn of the destruction, the loss of life, the horrors that have fallen on all our people, this beach of United State and American citizens will unite in grief against a common foe. Ourselves.

Chapter 14

Official Court Transcripts
4th Circuit Family Court, America
Pelham vs. Pelham
In the matter of custodial guardianship of five children:
Tammy Pelham, 17; Jacob Pelham, 10; Donald Pelham, 8;
Betsy Pelham, 4; and William Pelham, 2.

JUDGE: Mr. and Ms. Pelham. I want to thank you for your testimony. At this time, you will both be allowed to make a final statement. While I've already made my decision, these statements are given as a safeguard in case I've misjudged. If my decision stands, I will issue the verdict immediately. Mr. Pelham, you may begin.

JOHN PELHAM: Thank you, Judge. I was praying during the recess and I asked the good Lord to forgive me. This trial has shone a light on my weaknesses. First, I realize I do owe my wife an apology. Nancy, I'm sorry I slept with those other women. Now, you and I both know I wasn't getting what I should have been at home, but still, it wasn't right of me. Secondly, I haven't been paying enough attention to my kids. There are so many things in their lives I don't know about. And that's what's so great about this opportunity. If you grant me custody, Judge, you'll be giving me a second chance. A chance to really connect with my kids—to learn about their interests more and to help them through the challenges. I'm just devastated to hear about Jacob's eyes and I don't know why he never said anything when I was drilling him to catch fly balls. I just thought he wasn't focusing. I didn't know the boy was crippled. One of the guys at work has a retarded kid and I'm gonna make sure they meet each other, you know, to build that community you were talking about. And lastly, I'm horrified by the secrets my ex-wife has kept from me about Betsy. I don't much allow the mention of the devil in our house, and she's turning a blind eye when his shadow falls upon our darling baby girl. No sir, Judge. I will not tolerate that kind of behavior from any of my children. And if this was because of my neglect, well then, I'll surely have to pay. But I didn't know and she did. So you tell me, who's truly to blame.

Judge, I'm gonna work real hard to make sure my kids have everything they need. And if you tell me I can't hire that Russian girl then I'll find another person to help out. Shoot, I'll hire two. My mom will move in if she needs to. There ain't gonna be anything these kids won't have. And when Tammy comes back from school with a husband, I'm gonna make sure he treats her with the upmost respect.

My ex-wife has done tremendous harm to our family, but I'm gonna make it my sole mission in life to correct that harm. Thank you.

JUDGE: Thank you, Mr. Pelham. Ms. Pelham, you have the floor.

NANCY PELHAM: Judge, I'm rendered close to speechless. I had some remarks prepared but I'm afraid I can't let my ex-husband's comments go unanswered.

JUDGE: This is not a forum for debate, Ms. Pelham. Please stick to your prepared remarks.

NANCY PELHAM: Why... I... I have worked for the past seventeen years raising this family and there's another seventeen years of work still ahead. I'm not going to claim to have been perfect. I'm not that bold, nor should anyone else be. I've thought about this, and the real reason I don't consider being a mother a career is because you can change your career. You can walk away from a career. I can't change my children. I can't walk away from them. I'll always be their mother. And this is a burden I've taken on with all the joy and love the good Lord allows me. My life is plentiful and my children good.

We can talk about what John's done wrong and what I've done wrong. But in the end, Judge, I have been the primary parental figure for their entire lives. You would be doing the children a disservice by taking me away from them. It doesn't matter who you try and replace me with, be it John, his mother, or Albina, but the children will suffer from the loss of my guiding presence.

I'll say it again. I'm not perfect. I've made mistakes and I'll probably make many more. But in its own way, that's good too, isn't it? Children should know that their parents are flawed, because people are flawed. And shouldn't our children learn and understand this so they can build empathy with their peers? Isn't that important? I only want what's best for my children, and I don't doubt John wants the same. I can just do it better than he can, Judge. It's really that simple. I would be a better parent.

JUDGE: Thank you Ms. Pelham. I have listened very closely and with great interest to what you both have had to say. And were my duties different or had I been given authority, I would have overturned the judge who granted you a divorce. Obviously, there were things in that hearing I'm not allowed to know, but it is very clear to me that everyone in this family would have been better served had it remained intact. And to that point, I am issuing a letter to Judge Thompson, admonishing him for allowing the disintegration of this marriage, which has muddied this court and our society.

But my powers here are not that broad and I cannot overturn his verdict. As such, I am charged solely with the task of distributing custodial rights.

Ms. Pelham, your skills as a housewife are not in question here. This court can clearly see that you are an exceptional caretaker and housekeeper. And I have no doubt you love your children. However, you have been lost—morally ambiguous—for most, if not all of your adult life. And this court must consider the entirety of the children's environment. You've displayed a liberty with your thoughts and morals that are not becoming of a pure society.

Mr. Pelham, I'm very glad to hear that this trial has taught you a lesson. And I believe you have many more lessons to learn. Your strength and ability to provide for your children is important. But it is also important that you learn and grow from your mistakes so that you can show more discipline. Faith and spirituality are all well and good, but as you said so yourself, you can't achieve those without discipline.

Considering the evidence before me, and the wellbeing of these five children, I am granting full and exclusive custody to Mr. Pelham. This court finds Ms. Pelham an immediate danger to the wellness of her children. Her lack of morals and inconsistent behavior would present a toxic atmosphere for these young and highly impressionable minds. Ms. Pelham, you are right when you say community is important. Where you are so very wrong is in your understanding of that community. We are building a nation of strong citizens who aspire to perfection within the dictates of the Lord. Your ideas of humanity do not belong in such a society. And this court will not allow you to seed those ideas in the next generation. This court is adjourned.

Chapter 15

I'm sure you will read other accounts of this time. Most will give more details and analysis. I'm certainly not a historian. I'm simply a man with a job that gives him an abundance of time to ponder. And I wish for you, future people, something better than what we have now. And when I write that, I mean to say that I wish for you a better society, not necessarily a better life as individuals.

You see, that's where I think the trouble started. I think the people of the Old Country started holding their own individual selves above the goals of the whole. I'm told that this principle was the foundation of the nation from the beginning. They say there was a thing called the American Dream—as though a dream could actually be something tangible. And anyone who worked hard enough was rewarded with the American Dream. A few people collected their prize, while most did not. But the quest to achieve it, the endeavor to elevate one's individual self became the all-consuming mantra of the people.

This mentality initially survived in the Old Country because of the vast space the people enjoyed. The closer you live to your fellow citizen, the more communal your sensibilities must become. Plus, the founders established an intricate system of checks and balances that was meant to allow a culture of self-determination whilst setting up protections from tyranny—the greatest threat to any individualistic society. But when the people became obsessed with their own ideas, to the exclusion of rational contradiction, tyranny was welcomed as a tool to squash the opposition.

The moment the Old Country allowed their leaders to claim mandates when no majority was there, discredit the free press, label their political rivals *enemies*, appoint family members to high posts, and use force against peaceful assembly, tyranny had already arrived.

And that, in my opinion, is not only how the Second Civil War began but also what the war was about. It started by trying to evict tyranny and became a war about how to govern ourselves. That's probably very simplistic, I know. I'm fully aware that there are hundreds if not thousands of individual issues woven into this fabric of disagreement. But those had all been discussed, debated, challenged and legislated for over two hundred years using nothing more than a living document and profound respect—trust—for your fellow countryman. That system was working really well until we allowed tyranny a seat at the table. And he got his chair because we stopped trusting each other. No piece of paper can hold the burden of governance without the people's trust in one another.

It's easy for me, hidden away in a missile silo in the neutral Nation of Ute, to speculate on the folly of the others. My people and I are charged with two self-determined goals—maintain our own independence and maintain peace between our neighbors. And because of this, our perspective, while independent, lacks the depth one gets when indoctrinated into a society's moors. And because of this, we wouldn't fault someone from the United State or America if they called these scribbles ignorant. We're not afraid to be called out on our lack of knowledge or experience. We're not afraid to be contradicted by solid evidence or rigorous thought. We welcome the chance to understand an opposing point of view, even if it means our own ideas might shift because of it. The world is a marvelous place when we embrace diversity of thought, but can easily be destroyed by a collective myopia.

Dear reader, my eyes are fluttering. I'm seeing things. Reader, I don't want to write this, but it's happening. It's really happening. The red light is flashing. It's flashing. I've closed my eyes to make it stop, but it continues. It's flashing—one flash. It's sending a one flash signal. It's continuous, but I'm certain it's a one-flash signal. A map on the wall has illuminated. Sacramento and St. Louis. Those are the targets. Sacramento and St. Louis.

I can't bring myself to press the button. Not just yet. I want your counsel, future people. The world you're to inherit will change because of my action. I want you to counsel me. Tell me what to do! What kind of world do you want to live in? Reader—future person—if only you were here by my side and we could push this button together, or not. We could lock ourselves in here. Prevent the others from entering. Keep the buttons safe from being pressed. Or press them all and end this stalemate. Who do you want to be, future people? What kind of society will you build?

DIVISIBLE

by

Randy Anderson

About the Author

Randy is the author of five books. He began his literary adventure when he self-published his first book, On Making Off: Misadventures off off Broadway, a memoir of making theatre in New York City. His second book, Careful is a coming-of-age tale set in Ecuador. In 2016 he launched a time travel series called Time Phantom. The first two books, Amsterdam and Copenhagen are currently available. The third will be released later in 2017.

He is currently working on a literary trilogy where each book is a collection of short stories. This epic journey follows a disheartened baby boomer pastry chef through the second half of the last century.

Before writing books, Randy ran a small New York theater company from 1999-2004. During this time he produced over three-dozen productions and events. He was a co-producer of The Unconvention, a political theater festival during the 2004 Republican National Convention. Plays he's written include; New Year's Resolutions, Homelessness Homosexuals and Heretics, Testing Average, Kill The President, Armor of Wills, and The Dwelling.

47934854R00077

Made in the USA
San Bernardino, CA
11 April 2017